THE BROKEN AND THE BRAVE

VANESSA GRAY BARTAL

DRY CREEK PRESS

PROLOGUE

"Hey, pretty face. Back again?"

The waitress leaned over the counter, tipping her head and bestowing a friendly smile as she made her inspection.

"I can't get enough meatloaf," he said, but it wasn't the truth. The truth was that he couldn't get enough of her. Fresh-faced and blond with apple blossom cheeks and bright blue eyes, she wasn't his usual sort. Maybe that was why he was so captivated. She looked like the girl next door, but only if you lived next to a farm. That sold milk. And maybe cheese. She was not beautiful, not hot, but so adorable his eyes almost teared up every time he glanced at her. And he glanced a lot, so much it was shocking that she didn't seem to notice.

She had marked him as a pretty boy navy brat the minute he walked in, and maybe he was. The navy was his life, and it was possible he was a tad too into his bicep development, especially since becoming a SEAL. But for this girl, he'd be willing to set it all aside. *Smitten* was the correct term, and he was so far gone he hadn't said a word about her to any of his teammates. That was how he knew he meant it, because for the first time since joining the team, he found something he wanted to keep all to himself. Or rather someone.

The bell over the door chimed. His waitress turned to look and froze, blinking a couple of times. He regarded her look with jealousy because it was a look women usually bestowed on him. Not this girl, though. No matter how many hints he'd dropped, no matter how hard he flirted nothing ever came of it. He thought maybe she had a serious boyfriend, seeing as how she was a local. And either her boyfriend had just entered or he wasn't as good as he thought because she definitely had *the look,* and it definitely wasn't for him.

"So here's where you've been disappearing," a too-familiar voice said as a hand clapped him on the back, bestowing a knowing squeeze. The newcomer took the stool next to him and picked up a menu. "What's good?"

"I think he's partial to the meatloaf," the waitress said. *His* waitress. And now she was smiling shyly, not at him, but at the man to his right, his best friend.

"I can see why. Jay." He put down his menu and jutted his hand.

The waitress glanced at it a second before tentatively offering hers in return. "Jordan."

"And I guess you know my buddy here, Gaines." He was still holding Jordan's hand. Why was he still holding Jordan's hand? Gaines stared at their combined hands, his overheated imagination picturing the arcs of electricity being traded back and forth.

Jordan glanced at him, distracted. "Actually no. I never learned his name. Hello, Gaines. Nice to finally meet you." She finally withdrew her hand from Jay and offered it to him.

Gaines took her hand, noting its softness, its delicate smallness compared to his. He gave her his best smile, one that usually worked wonders, but it was lost on her; her attention had already returned to Jay.

"I guess I'll have the meatloaf," Jay said, eyes never leaving Jordan's.

"I guess I'll go get it," she said, but she made no move to turn away.

Gaines sighed and made a mental note of the exact moment his hopes and dreams imploded and turned to dust.

CHAPTER 1

Gaines "Ribs" Hillcrest learned early not to ring the doorbell. One or both of the kids might be sleeping, and Jordan would kill him if he woke them. But when no one answered his knock, he wasn't sure what to do. He knew they were home; he could hear them. But no one answered the repeated taps. His hand hovered uncertainly over the bell, and then he decided to test the handle. *Unlocked.* Should he…Too late to ponder, he had already let himself inside. And then he wished he could undo it because he heard something he was unaccustomed to hearing, yelling.

"It's my *job,* Jordan. I can't help that it's my *job.*"

"Stop saying it's your job, Jay. I know it's your job. I've been living with your *job* for twelve years."

"And resenting it all that time," Shimmer said.

Jordan gasped. "That is not true, that is absolutely not true. How dare you say that? I have been nothing if not supportive, but I'm tired, Jay, and when you're here, you're not really here…"

"I can't believe you are heaping this on me. If you can't keep up at home while I'm away, that's on you."

Ribs was shocked by the unprecedented ugliness. He'd never heard Shimmer or Jordan talk this way before, and especially not to each other. *Stay or go,* he wondered. Squeezing his eyes closed and mustering some courage, he took a breath and stepped into the room.

"Hey, guys. No one answered the door, so I let myself in." His tone was overly bright, especially in contrast to the heavy tension now simmering in the kitchen. Shimmer and Jordan looked at him, equal parts shocked and embarrassed.

"I've got to pack," Shimmer said before stalking from the room.

Jordan swiped her fingers under her eyes and forced a wobbly smile. "Hey, sorry."

"Where are the kids?"

"With Amelia," Jordan said. Her eyes were still leaking. She pressed her fingers beneath them, lip wobbling.

"Jordy, is everything okay?"

"You caught us at a bit of a bad time," Jordan admitted, aiming for a smile and failing mightily.

"I'm sorry," Ribs said, glancing helplessly for the door. "I could go, come back when Amelia gets here with the kids."

"Hey, no, absolutely not." She reached out and gave his sleeve a little tug, finding a real smile. "We love having you here, you know that. You're always welcome. I'm sorry it's so…"

"It's okay," he said, offering what he hoped was a reassuring smile. Her eyes flooded and she looked away, fighting for composure. "Maybe I'll go see what he's up to, help him pack and whatnot."

"You guys are packing pros," she said with a watery little sniffle.

"Undefeated," he agreed. It would have been natural to give her shoulder a squeeze or pat, but he went by without reaching out, leaving her untouched. With Jordan he always had to check himself, to fight upriver of his natural instincts, in case too much came spilling out, overwhelming them both. He'd fought hard to keep his secret these thirteen years. For all their sakes, he planned to take it to the grave.

Shimmer was in their bedroom, roughly tossing things into his bag.

"Need any help?" Ribs asked.

In reply, Shimmer barked a harsh laugh. Ribs's eyes landed on the bed and he gave a low whistle. "Is Jordan in some kind of competition for the most throw pillows? If so, I think she's winning."

"I dunno," Shimmer replied, sounding as miserable as he looked.

"What's up?" Ribs asked. He tossed a handful of pillows onto the floor and plopped onto the bed, letting his feet dangle over the edge. He'd taken off his shoes, but it still felt weird to put his feet in anyone else's bed, even his closest friends.

Shimmer stopped throwing things in his case long enough to glare at him. "It's just...everything. She's so..." he waved helplessly in the direction of Jordan.

"It's a rough patch," Ribs said.

"It's been a rough patch since the kids came along, and I'm sick of it. I can't be here twenty four seven helping out if I'm off making the money. It's not like she works."

"I thought you guys agreed you want her to stay home while the kids are little," Ribs reminded him. Back when Jordan was pregnant the first time, Shimmer had gushed over their plans. *Jordy's going to quit and raise the babies. She wants to be that mom, you know? The one who makes all the cupcakes and homemade Play-Doh.*

"Yeah, but she can't have it both ways. She was going to stay home while I worked, that was the deal. Now she wants me to do everything —work the crazy job then be a fulltime parent. It's impossible." He tossed a pair of boxers in his bag with disgust. "I'm so over this."

Ribs scowled. This felt like more than blowing off steam. This felt bad. "What? What are you saying?"

Shimmer picked up the pair of underwear he'd just discarded and rolled them into a compact ball. "Exactly what I said. I'm over this. I think maybe we need a break."

"You do not need a break. You're fine."

"You don't know," Shimmer said. "You have no idea what it's like to be married, how hard it is. I'm tired of it, the constant nagging and complaining. Nothing I do is ever enough. She's impossible to please. Maybe we were too young when we got married."

Ribs sat up because it wasn't the kind of discussion you could have lying down. "Jay, stop. Breathe. Something's been not right with you for months, and this is a side effect of that. What is going on, really? Are you okay?"

"I'm fine. I'm not the problem here, it's her."

It was on the tip of Ribs's tongue to disagree, but he bit it. Now was not the time to come to Jordan's defense. "I'm sure marriage is hard, I'm sure it takes work, but you can't throw away twelve years over a little rough spot. That's not you. You'll regret it, I know you. After this assignment, we'll go out for a night, talk, see where it stands and what we can find to help, okay? But promise you won't do anything rash, won't throw away a lifetime of love in a moment of anger."

Shimmer nodded, but he still looked far away and unreachable. Ribs had seen that look before, and it scared him. He stood and gripped his bicep. "Hey, listen. Things get messed up in here." He tapped his brain. "Doesn't mean they're real or true. We love you, all of us, and we're here for you. We'll get this figured out, okay?"

He nodded and let out a shaky breath. The hard set of his shoulders relaxed and he glanced toward the kitchen with something like regret. "I guess I should go say goodbye before I go wheels up."

"Sounds like a good idea," Ribs said. He reached for the throw pillows he'd tossed on the floor, trying and failing to rearrange them the perfect way Jordan had them.

Shimmer paused at the edge of the room and regarded him with an inscrutable stare. "Take care of her for me, okay?"

"Always," Ribs said, tone flippant as he stared at the round pillow in his hand. It wasn't an odd comment for Shimmer to make, not in their world. They often made those sorts of requests and promises to each other over their wives, kids, girlfriends, mothers. It wasn't until much later he'd remember and allow the request to play itself over and over in his head, tormenting him with all the other things he could have said and done.

CHAPTER 2

"Why are you touching my pillows?" Jordan hovered at the edge of the room, observing Ribs a few seconds unseen. He was a seriously beautiful man, with features far more perfect than Jay's. Jay had a sweet face, was more cute than handsome. Ribs had intimidated her from that first day he entered the café, not like Jay who had felt real and touchable from the get go.

Ribs jumped, accidentally launching the pillow into the air. "I lack the correct chromosome to know how to arrange these."

"Thank goodness, from women everywhere," Jordan said. She entered the room, swept the mass of pillows onto the floor, and plopped onto the bed, patting the space beside her in one motion.

Ribs eyed the bed warily, as if he wasn't certain he should join her, and Jordan bit back a laugh. *As if he would ever see her that way, his best friend's ordinary little wife.* Ribs was like Ethan, and the Ethans and Ribs of the worlds always dated the Amelias of the world, women so spectacularly beautiful and put together they made you wonder if they were retired supermodels or genetically modified by the FDA. Women who could make you feel old, chubby, and frumpy in comparison, if you let them. For Jordan, it was a daily struggle not to let them, at least since having the kids.

At last Ribs overcame any misgivings or hesitation and stretched out beside her, not that they were in any way touching. The bed was king size, plenty enough room for them to maintain a safe distance. *Plenty enough room for Jay to curl into a ball away from me, night after night, shutting himself off, never crossing the barrier I desperately need him to cross.*

Think about something else, anything but your marriage. "Please tell me you're staying for supper. I made a ton."

"Yes, please," Ribs said, rubbing his tummy in an unconscious gesture that made her smile. Jordan liked to think she provided the wholesome stability in his otherwise glamorous life. He might be a globetrotting playboy spy, but she fed him real food and provided an anchor, a home base she hoped also acted as a touchstone for him, somewhere real and tangible where he was loved and cared for. She'd been married into the navy long enough to realize how important that was. No matter where he went or how far he traveled, she always wanted him to know he had a place to call home, that he always had them.

"The kids are going to be stoked. Amelia and Ethan are staying, too." She yawned and covered it with the back of her hand.

"What time are they getting here?" Ribs asked. He sounded strangely tense, and she thought she knew why. Obviously the fight between her and Jay had disturbed him, like hearing your parents argue. Would it make him feel better if she told him how common those fights were now? Probably not.

"Not sure, but soon." She yawned again, but she couldn't help it. The baby was teething molars, keeping her up most nights, unwilling to wean even though Jordan was desperately ready to stop nursing. She loved her babies, loved nurturing them with milk she made for that purpose, but her body hadn't been her own in far too long. Was that part of the problem with Jay? Did he see her as a mother instead of a wife the way she did? It was hard to feel sexy with a baby gnawing you at three AM.

"You should nap," Ribs said.

"I have so much to do," Jordan said, baleful glance sliding toward the kitchen and laundry room where piles of work awaited.

Ribs reached over and poked her, drawing her attention back to him. "Sleep, Jordy, I command you."

He was so ornery she couldn't help but grin at him. "Well, if you command me, obviously I have to obey."

"At long last, that actually worked on a woman," he said.

She laughed, and it was the last thing she remembered before she closed her eyes.

*R*ibs watched her sleep a few minutes like the pathetic loser he was. He was deeply worried, about both her and Shimmer. Basking in their epic love story had been painful, but manageable because he so desperately wanted happiness for both of them. But if their marriage broke up, that would be the worst sort of pain he could imagine, for all of them. Everyone would expect him to take Shimmer's side because they were tight, but Ribs honestly didn't know what he would do. He couldn't imagine his life without Jordan. She'd become important to him over the years, as much as anyone in his life. They were friends, too, and she had made it a point to take care of him. Never in a weird or inappropriate way, never in a way that circumvented Shimmer. But she always invited him over when he was in town, took an interest in his wellbeing, and sent him packages when he was away, ones that were filled with homemade treats and pictures drawn by Charlotte, their oldest daughter. By now his fridge probably had almost as much of her artwork on it as theirs did, and he loved it. She and Shimmer were both family to him, and if they broke up…

They won't break up, he assured himself. When Shimmer got back, he would talk some sense into him. They all would, the whole team. Everyone had a vested interest in their marriage, not just Ribs. Shimmer was the first one to get married, had been married when they were newbie SEALs, far before anyone else on the team was ready to settle down. It was only now that the other guys were beginning to hit their thirties and pair off like the world was ending.

Not you, though, that mean little voice inside him said.

Someday, he reassured himself, forcing his eyes toward the ceiling and away from Jordan. It wasn't his unrequited crush on Jordan that had kept him from settling down over the years. Rather it was a combination of factors. And he knew enough about life and relationships to understand that his crush wasn't in the same realm as her and Shimmer's relationship. There was the very real possibility that if she had chosen him instead all those years ago, they wouldn't have worked out. In fact there was a high probability that would be the case. Jordan had long been his dream girl, and that was where she had always remained, in the realm of dreams and fantasy. What she and Shimmer had was real. Ribs had watched it up close for more than a decade now. There had been times, including today, when he didn't think he had the stomach for what they went through. She was an escapist fantasy and since that first day he had never, ever once pictured himself in Shimmer's place. Never envied in a tangible way what they had. Rather he had felt protective of it on both their behalves. He had kept an eye on Shimmer when they were on assignment, wanting to make certain he remained faithful to the vows he'd made, to himself and to Jordan. Not that Shimmer had ever required a keeper. He'd been faithful, always. Had never partaken in even harmless flirting with another woman. He had been as devoted as a husband can be to his wife and family.

That devotion, Ribs now realized, had been a blessing to him as well. Because what if he hadn't been so devoted? What if he'd cheated on Jordan, used the massive amount of time he spent away from home to run around and sow his wild oats? How would Ribs's feelings toward both of them have been different? Would his feelings for Jordan have shifted into something more protective, more predatory? Would he have felt more entitled to push his agenda if he knew Shimmer was running around and being unfaithful?

Thankfully he had never found out. *And I never will,* he told himself, needing reassured again. When Shimmer got back, they would have a talk, a long talk about what was going on. Ribs would make certain everything was on the up and up, for both their sakes. Because if Shimmer ever cheated on Jordan…

Without his permission, his face swiveled toward her, taking in the soft set of her sweet features. With effort, his eyes turned back toward the ceiling. It was a moot point, and it would remain a moot point. Or else.

The doorbell rang and he jumped. Jordan didn't stir, and he was glad. He almost expected to hear the baby cry before remembering the kids were with Amelia. He jumped off the bed and skittered down the hall, yanking open the door before the bell could chime again.

"Hey," Ethan said, not sounding at all surprised to see him there. In his arms he held three-year-old Charlotte who was asleep on his shoulder. Beside him stood his wife, Amelia, holding 12 month old Nash who looked fussy and unhappy to see all of them.

"Mama," he declared unhappily, starting to cry.

"Shh, shh, shh," Amelia soothed, doing that bouncy sway thing that seemed to come naturally to every woman on the planet. "It's okay, we're home. We're here now."

"Jordy's asleep," Ribs whispered. "Hey, buddy," he added to Nash, giving him a little nudge that made him shy away and cry harder. It was likely the baby didn't remember him, which was a shame since he'd actually been in town on the day of his birth. He was the first person to hold him, after Shimmer and Jordan, of course. They'd all three sat on the bed, Jordan between them looking ridiculously beautiful for a woman who'd endured twelve hours of labor with an eight pound baby. Shimmer'd had his arm around Jordan while Ribs sat on her other side, both of them beaming at him as he held their boy.

"He's perfect," Ribs said and meant it. He never understood why people said babies were beautiful, until Charlotte and Nash came along. And he thought they were more beautiful than other babies he'd seen, not that he was biased. Or maybe he was, but he didn't care. They were perfect.

"It's about time you procured one of these for yourself," Jordan had said.

"You're not supposed to be so articulate this late in the day," he'd returned.

"Don't badger him, Jordy. He's not ready," Shimmer had said. "He'll have to live vicariously through us."

"Uncle Ribs," Jordan had said, giving him a sleepy smile, her head resting on Shimmer's shoulder.

Uncle Ribs he remained, though the kids barely knew, a testament to how often he came and went in their lives. Somehow despite leaving the navy, he and Shimmer still seemed to travel as much, maybe more.

If the kids barely know me, how much do they know their dad? Ribs wondered before shooing the stray thought away.

Nash was really working up a howl. "I think he wants to nurse," Amelia said. "I hate to wake Jordan, but I'm sure she wouldn't want him to get this upset." She bypassed the men and headed to Jordan's room. Ribs nodded his head toward the kitchen, inviting Ethan to follow. He deposited Charlotte on the couch and pulled a blanket over her before heading toward the kitchen.

"That kid can sleep through anything," Ethan noted.

"Like Jordan," Ribs said, then pressed his lips together. It was weird to know the sleep habits of a woman not your wife, but he'd spent enough time with Shimmer and Jordan to know that once Jordan was out, she was out. Good luck to Amelia trying to wake her now.

Ethan didn't comment on the lapse, merely opened a cupboard and helped himself to a glass. All of them had a certain level of comfort with each other's houses and families. It was the nature of their long and close connection that they felt a kinship that surpassed friendship, sometimes even surpassed family. They had seen and done things together, unspeakable things that bonded them in unfathomable ways. For life.

"Where's Shimmer?" Ethan asked. He opened the fridge and spied its contents, trying to find something drinkable among Jordan's healthy choices.

"Wheels up," Ribs said.

Ethan whirled toward him with a scowl. "What? No."

"Yeah, I watched him pack."

Ethan set down his glass. "I'm privy to his itinerary. He's not wheels up until tomorrow."

"Then where did he go? And why?" Ribs voiced the questions both of them were thinking. They stared at each other, sharing a frown. It was never good when a military guy began keeping secrets. It could only mean one of two things: either he was cheating on his wife or headed for a breakdown.

"Maybe we should call Ridge, put a trace on him," Ethan suggested.

"Something's not right with him. When I got here…" he paused and looked toward the door to make certain they were still alone. "He was reaming Jordan. Bad."

"That doesn't sound like them," Ethan said.

Ribs shook his head. "He said…he said he wants out."

Ethan froze, wide eyed. "He said that to Jordan?"

"To me. I told him to hold off and we'll talk about it when he gets back. But if he hurts her…"

He didn't realize his fists were clenched until Ethan tossed a piece of ice at him, letting it ping painfully off his forehead. "You'll do nothing because it's their marriage and not your business."

"But…"

"Not your business, Gaines. I know you and Jordan are…close. All the more reason to tread carefully here. You don't want chatter."

The military/espionage circle was close, small, and tight-knit. That made it a combustible combination for gossip. "Is there chatter?"

"There's always been chatter," Ethan said with a sigh, taking a sip of his drink, what looked to be some kind of green juice that made him grimace before taking another gulp.

"What kind of chatter? What do they say?"

"The usual. That you spend an awful lot of time here, that you and Jordan seem unusually close, that Shimmer must be an awfully understanding guy to let you so near his wife."

"What?" Ribs exclaimed. "I am never here without him."

Ethan quirked a brow at him.

Ribs sighed, annoyed. "Except now. This is the first time in forever I've been here solo. I'm always with Shimmer or we're a trio."

Ethan shrugged. "Not saying I give it any credence, merely passing the info along. And warning you. This is their relationship, not yours. Tread carefully and keep your nose out." He tipped his glass toward Ribs before downing the rest of the green juice and grimacing again.

"I'm never here," Ribs insisted, running his hand through his hair. He felt an odd mix of righteous indignation and a whole lot of guilt. He and Jordan hadn't done anything, ever, not once. Not a surreptitious touch, word, or even glance. But apparently someone was privy to his secret thoughts and desires, the ones that made him squirm with shame for being unable to control feelings he didn't want to have.

"Probably a good thing," Ethan said. He held up his glass and stared at it. "This stuff grows on you."

"Probably, if you drink enough," Ribs agreed. He didn't try to disagree with Ethan because what was the point? Part of being brothers meant you were real with each other, warts and all. He'd never admitted his secret feelings for Jordan, but he'd never had to. Everyone but Shimmer seemed to have guessed. Or had he? *Take care of her.*

What had that meant? Ribs pushed it away before he could think too much or peer too closely.

CHAPTER 3

Jordan entered, Nash in her arms and still wailing, Charlotte strangling her legs and also joining the cacophony. Amelia trailed helplessly behind, trying to calm one or both of the kids.

"Hey, buddy," Ethan tried, reaching for Nash while Ribs knelt next to Charlotte, trying to coax a smile. Absently he wondered if a love of children ran proportionate to testosterone because he and all of his buddies loved kids. In fact he couldn't think of one guy who didn't love them, even the ones who were averse to commitment went gooey at the sight of a cute baby.

No such luck, though. The kids wanted their mother and only their mother who currently looked close to tears herself.

"New idea: Jordan can tend to the kids and we can get supper," Amelia said, taking charge. She bypassed them and began setting things out. Ethan joined her, opening a drawer to find hot pads. Jordan sat and pulled both kids into her arms.

"Can I get you anything?" Ribs asked her, still kneeling from his attempt to woo Charlotte.

"No," she said, tossing him a distracted smile as she rubbed the baby's back and patted Charlotte. "They don't spend a lot of time away from me. I think maybe it was a little traumatizing."

"Where's Daddy?" Charlotte wailed.

"He had to go to work," Jordan said. Ribs heard the weariness in her tone and hid his wince. She was exhausted, had been exhausted since Charlotte was born, and where was Shimmer?

He'd better have a good excuse for dodging his family, and it had better not involve another woman, Ribs thought, reaching for his phone.

"Guess what? I have a video of Smokey on here." Last time he was in town they went to Ridge and Maggie's house for supper. The kids went wild for their dog, Smokey, who loved them in turn. Ribs had grabbed a video, with a prescient understanding that he might need to use it to impress them. Today they weren't impressed, but they did stop crying as he pulled up the video and turned it to face them.

Thank you, Jordan mouthed, tossing him a tired smile. He realized, belatedly, that she always looked tired lately. Her eyes were shadowed, rims red. An air of heaviness and exhaustion radiated off her and he wondered when she'd last slept a full night.

Ethan's eyes burned a hole in him, and he refused to look because he already knew he was treading dangerously. Not with his nearness to Jordan and the kids, there was nothing untoward or unusual in that. He'd always been hands-on, willing to pick them up, read to them, change diapers. But there was something new there, something that had never happened before—a simmering resentment toward Shimmer and his absence. Ribs had never taken sides before, and now that he had he realized he was squarely in Jordan's camp. She was clearly drowning, being pulled under by the heavy weight of motherhood, and where was her husband? Not working like he said, and that was ominous.

I need space, Ribs thought, forcing himself to take a breath because he knew Ethan was right. No good would come of putting himself in their marriage. For twelve years he had managed to keep the proper space and distance. Messing that up now would only end in pain for everyone.

His phone beeped. The kids whimpered when he paused the video of Smokey to check it. "It'll just take a second," he promised as he glanced at the text, coincidentally from Smokey's owner, Ridge.

Are you available for an assignment?

Ridge wasn't his boss, but they worked in the same interchangeable realm, enabling Ribs to take the odd assignment when Ridge needed another hand. It was usually something that needed kid gloves and the thought of something Ribs could sink his teeth into had never been more welcome.

Yes. What's up?

Jones. Got a situation. Go forth and be tropical.

Ribs smiled as he flicked the screen back to the video of Smokey. They'd all piled on Jones when he took the cushy job on a remote island, but now Ribs was glad. Getting away and clearing his head had never felt more appealing. By the time he returned, he was certain Jordan and Shimmer would have sorted their problems. And if they didn't, it was still no business of his.

His eyes flicked to Jordan as she lovingly caressed Nash's neck, kissing the top of his head and pausing to inhale his baby scent. His heart kicked and he turned away. *No business of mine. None whatsoever. I'm sure wherever Shimmer is, he has a good reason.*

"*Y*ou did what?" After the Jones situation was sorted and settled, Ribs returned to work and arranged a lunch with Shimmer, hoping to touch base and get some answers, if only about where he went when he left for his assignment a day early.

"I got a vasectomy." As if to drive the point home, Shimmer slid his finger across his throat in a motion of finality.

"Without telling Jordan?" Ribs said, aghast. Granted he wasn't married, but even he knew it was the sort of thing husbands and wives were supposed to discuss.

Shimmer shrugged. "She'd been getting that look in her eye again, the I-want-a-baby look the last few weeks. Had to be done."

"I don't understand," Ribs said slowly.

Shimmer let out a breath and swiped a hand wearily over his face. "Look, I've been doing a lot of thinking, okay? That first decade, when it was only me and Jordan, things were fire. And then the kids came along and everything changed."

"You love your kids," Ribs insisted.

"I do," Shimmer said earnestly. "But having them took a battering ram to our relationship. Nothing has been the same since. Jordan is exhausted all the time, the kids always come first. We can't get a break, a minute to think, let alone…" He broke off and shook his head. "She's not rational when it comes to babies. Someday she'll agree this was the right decision. We're done, we need to be done."

Ribs didn't reply, but he had grave doubts. Knowing Jordan as he did, she wouldn't take kindly to Shimmer making such a massive life decision without her input. And knowing how much she loved her kids—despite her ongoing exhaustion—learning she would never have another would be a blow, probably a big one.

"What are you going to do when she's ready to start trying and magically can't get pregnant again?" Ribs asked.

Shimmer faltered, frowning. "I'll face that when we get there. In the meantime I'll start prepping her, slipping in things about needing to be done, that kind of stuff. Maybe she'll agree with me and it won't even be an issue." He picked up his cup and took a drink while Ribs stared at him. He was concerned and uncertain but, as he'd so recently reminded himself, this wasn't his business. At least Shimmer wasn't running around on Jordan. That was a massive relief, even if an entirely new set of issues had been unleashed.

Not my problem, Ribs reminded himself. "How are things otherwise? With you, I mean. You've seemed a little…off or something the last few months."

"Nah," Shimmer said, shrugging off his concern. "It's been a lot, you know, with Jordan and the kids and work. Normal stuff, nothing I can't handle. Tell me about Jones and the girl."

"You should have seen Jonesie with her, it was hilarious."

Shimmer smiled, the first real smile Ribs had seen in a while. "Start from the beginning and tell me everything. Is the job as cushy as we imagine?"

"Cushier," Ribs said, leaning in as he really got in to his story.

They ended lunch on a good note, the best encounter they'd had in months, if not years. It made Ribs realize an odd sort of tension had crept between them. He had no idea what it was or where it had come from, but he was relieved it now felt gone. Maybe fatherhood had weighed even heavier than Ribs realized. Maybe the relief of taking the possibility of another off the table had fixed everything, not only between Jordan and Shimmer but with Shimmer himself.

Whatever the reason, Ribs felt optimistic as they said goodbye, not only for Shimmer but for his relationship with Jordan, too. They were solid and committed; whatever issues they had, they would work them out, he was certain. As the best friend, he'd be on standby to make certain. Or at least whenever he was around, which wasn't often these days. Someday they'd all be old and retired and they'd have more time. Until then, he was always on standby, a part time friend with a fulltime kind of love.

That's pretty good, I should write it down, he thought, smiling as he jogged to his car.

Later he would remember it as the last good day in a seemingly unending nightmare.

CHAPTER 4

"There you are. Cheater."

His team member, Eliza, greeted him with a pouty frown. She'd been in petulant meltdown mode since his return from Jones's island.

"He's still tan," his other team member, Logan, added.

"Guys, I couldn't pick my team. If so, I obviously would have taken you with me. Look at you both, so pasty. The island sun would have done wonders," Ribs said, making them frown harder.

"It's not that you went without us," Eliza said.

"Yes, it is. Shut up. You went to paradise without us," Logan accused.

"It's who you worked with," Eliza continued undaunted, ignoring him. "Them. The others."

"We're all on the same side," Ribs reminded her. There was a bit of competition between teams, and Ribs got it. Ridge's team tended to get the high profile assignments, and they always nailed them. Ribs's team tended to get the leftovers. (And they nailed them, but it seemed to matter less.) Since Ridge was his former team leader, he felt less competitive about it than the others who didn't have that sort of mentor/subordinate relationship to rely on. To them, Ridge's team was the favored chosen one while theirs all too often got the shaft.

"Tell me one thing," Eliza pled, clasping her hands together under her chin. "Did Blue mention me?"

"You know he's married," Logan reminded her with a grimace. "To The Colonel's daughter." Quickly, his head darted side to side, the natural motion everyone did after mentioning The Colonel, as if he would hear and know and, more terrifying, suddenly show up.

Eliza grimaced. "I don't have a *crush* on him. Gross. I'm a fan of his work, have been for a decade since I first learned to code. The man is legend." She kissed her fingers and released them into the air.

"He didn't mention you," Ribs said. "But I'm sure he was thinking about you and feeling intimidated by all your gains lately." He motioned to the massive wall of computers behind her.

Mollified, she turned and gave the computers a loving stare, too.

"You said gains and your name is Gaines," Logan nodded. "You're, like, a master of ceremonies or something. Barnum and Bailey, dropping the rhymes."

"Are you under the impression that Barnum and Bailey were rappers?" Ribs asked.

"Weren't they?" Logan asked, so deadpan it was hard to know if he was joking.

"Maybe we should get to work," Ribs said, eyeing him cautiously. He and Eliza were both still firmly in their twenties and Ribs was beginning to feel like the old man in the group. It didn't help that Jones, one of the only other bachelor holdouts in their group, had now found love. *I should go on a date or something,* Ribs thought but pushed it away before it could take root. Someday he'd get around to finding someone special. Until then he had a job to do.

He worked steadily for a few hours until his phone rang. He glanced down, confused to see Ridge's name staring back at him. Ridge was a diehard texter, reserving phone conversations for earth shattering things. *Maybe Maggie is pregnant again,* Ribs thought. Since their baby was still a newborn, that would definitely be earth shattering.

"What's up?" he asked, in lieu of a greeting.

There was a pause, the sort of pause that said more than words, and Ribs gripped the phone tighter, dread filling his chest. Too many years in the military and intelligence had taught him what that pause meant. He sucked a deep breath and held it.

Ridge swallowed hard and spoke, his voice a rough rasp. "It's Shimmer."

*There was some back and forth about who would tell Jordan. Ridge felt like he should. Their former team leader, he still felt the weight of responsibility for all of them.

Ethan thought he should, given Amelia's strong friendship with Jordan and her kids.

In the end, everyone agreed Ribs should be the one. Early on as newbie SEALs, he and Shimmer formed their own sub-unit, a close friendship that never dimmed with time. When Jordan came along, they became a trio. The three of them were close, so close everyone agreed the news should come from him. Ribs agreed, but he had never dreaded a task more.

He left work immediately and drove straight to her house, hoping to prevent the gossip network before it reached her. Soon the other wives would start to show up with casseroles, assuming she knew because their husbands knew. The truth was she would probably be one of the last to know. For that reason it was imperative to arrive before someone well meaning texted her, alerting her before he could do it in person. And still he lingered, white knuckling his steering wheel, gritting his teeth together, pushing back the tears that clogged his throat. Now was not the time to fall apart; that could happen after he'd seen to Jordan.

With a deep breath, he forced himself to leave the car and stride toward the house. The walkway had never felt so long, the house so far away. Usually he jogged the few steps from his car to the house, anxious to get inside and see his friends and their children. Today each step was filled with leaden anxiety.

He knocked lightly, in case the baby was sleeping. Jordan must have been nearby because she opened the door and beamed at him.

"Hey, it's the magic time of day when both kids are napping. Come in and have a cup of coffee." She grabbed his hand, clasping it as she used it to tug him inside. She turned toward the kitchen but his feet planted in the entryway, pulling her back. She stopped short and swiveled to face him, the expression on her face slipping from amusement to confusion to horror with lightning speed. She put both hands over her mouth, shaking her head furiously as she took a step back.

He opened his mouth and took a breath.

"Don't," she croaked. "Don't say it."

If he didn't say it, it wouldn't be true, he got that. But denial wouldn't change anything. "Jordy," he said, all the misery that was in him contained in that one word and she went down, collapsing like an unsteady high rise. Her knees buckled and she would have smacked the wood if Ribs hadn't caught her, arms reaching out and grasping her, pulling her close against him as he sank with her.

They melted into a combined puddle on the floor, she half in his lap and sobbing, great wracking sobs that shook her body so all he could do was hold on, bestow whatever strength he could. He was all that held her upright. She gave him her full weight as everything within her turned inside, trying and failing to absorb the shock.

For forty minutes they remained that way, long after his feet and legs went numb, long after his arms started to ache and her tears went dry. She had what he would call sobbing dry heaves. Her body still shook with them as a sound of unearthly pain wrenched from her throat, but the tears were gone. It must have been intensely painful, but she seemed unable to stop. Ribs didn't say a word in all that time, merely held her and petted her and rocked her.

And then the kids woke up, first one crying and then the other. And that penetrated. Jordan sat up and shook her head as if waking from a dream. She dashed at her eyes, eyes that were dry and swollen and red, and sniffled pathetically.

"Want me to get them?" Ribs offered.

"I've got this," Jordan said softly. With a shaky breath, she peeled herself off the floor and went to get her children.

CHAPTER 5

Amelia and Ethan and Ridge and Maggie showed up together, bearing food. No one was hungry, except maybe the kids, but Maggie doled food anyway. And everyone ate, regardless of the fact that everything tasted like sawdust.

Jordan fussed over the kids, making certain their food was arranged and cut just so, their cups filled with milk, their chairs arranged properly at the table.

Maggie set a plate before her and she stared at it as if unable to fathom what to do with it.

"Try to take a few bites," Amelia urged, rubbing her back gently.

Jordan nodded and dutifully picked up her fork.

Charlotte chattered nonstop throughout the meal, which was a blessing for everyone because no one was ready to talk yet. The shock was still too palpable. She asked questions about Smokey. Maggie and Ridge took turns showing her pictures and videos on their phone.

"Can we get a doggie, Mommy?" Charlotte asked, turning wide eyed toward Jordan.

"We'll ask Da..." Jordan began before breaking off midsentence and staring into space, the shock hitting her anew.

"Maybe we could start with a doggie stuffed animal," Ribs

suggested. "Something to practice on so you can show your mom how good you are at taking care of it."

Charlotte nodded, eyes brimming with excitement.

"Here, you pick out the one you want, and I'll buy it today. It will be here in a couple of days," Ribs said, handing her his phone. He had no qualms about her knowing how to use it. Everyone under the age of five these days seemed born already knowing how to implement technology.

Frog and his wife showed up. Ribs let them in and answered a call from Jones who was planning to fly home as soon as possible. When he returned to the kitchen, Amelia and Maggie were cleaning up while Ridge held his baby and Ethan held Nash. Charlotte brought Ribs's phone to him and crawled into his lap.

"This one, I want this one," she said, pointing to the dog she'd selected. It was a giant stuffed dog from some German company that cost three hundred dollars. Unbidden, he barked a short laugh. Everyone paused their dreariness to smile at him, except Jordan who bit her lip, concerned.

"You don't ha…" she started, but he cut her off with a wave of his hand.

"Absolutely yes, it's perfect." He pushed the button and ordered it. Charlotte ran off to get paper and a couple of crayons, either to draw a picture of the dog or to draw a welcome picture, he wasn't certain.

Thank you, Jordan mouthed.

He smiled and leaned forward to squeeze her hand. She gripped it like a lifeline, grasping it tightly between both hers with a shudder, telling him her act of holding herself together was merely that, an act.

He stood and pulled her up beside him, shepherding her from the room with an arm around her shoulders. She allowed him to lead her down the hall and to her bedroom. They sat on the edge and she unleashed again, sobbing with a fresh wave of tears as she pressed her face to his chest and held on tight.

These tears came to a natural and healthier end, slowly dwindling to sniffles. She leaned her ear tiredly against his chest.

"How?" she whispered.

He took a steadying breath and squeezed his eyes closed, not wanting to tell her. She both wanted and needed to hear it, however. "They found his car in an abandoned lot by the river. One shot in the head."

She paused, absorbing that. "Murder?"

He paused, forcing the word through rubbery lips. "No."

She darted off the bed and into the bathroom, heaving into the toilet until there was nothing left. Ribs stood beside her, hand pressed to her back to keep her steady. When she was finished he wetted a cloth and pressed it to her forehead.

"Thank you," she said as she sank wearily to the tile.

He sat gingerly beside her, out of words, out of everything. Later there would be time to talk, to pick apart the details and figure out where everything went wrong. But for now it was enough to sit and be. Sharing the misery of grief together somehow took a weight off both of them. Jordan leaned against him and he put his arm around her, resting his head companionably on hers.

An unknown time later, Amelia arrived with Nash. "Sorry, but this guy's getting pretty adamant about wanting his mama." She handed Nash to Jordan. Immediately he clutched at her and started to root, whimpering to nurse. Ribs started to get to his feet, but Jordan grabbed his forearm.

"Just stay. Please."

He sank down and put his arm back around her. She leaned against him while Nash nursed, so noisily and cheerfully that they laughed. "Kids are the best," she whispered, sighing.

"Your kids, maybe," he agreed, giving her a squeeze.

They sat in companionable silence a few minutes before Jordan sat up, staring at him in alarm. "I have to call his parents and my mom."

"I can call his parents," Ribs offered.

"Shouldn't I be the one?" she asked.

"I've known them as long, and they'll understand."

She sat back, relieved. "My mom is going to want to come."

"Sorry," he said.

She giggled and shook her head. "That's terrible. But true. I just… don't know how to do this. There's everything, absolutely everything."

"Take it a minute at a time, and we'll help. We have resources to sort through all the legalities and insurance, so we'll work on that. Amelia and Maggie will set you up with meals. Everything else we'll deal with as it comes, okay?" He paused and took a breath, tamping down his own emotions. "He had a plan, right? For the burial and service and everything?" They'd all done it as newbie SEALs, given the high likelihood of their deaths. It was only practical. Shimmer's danger level hadn't diminished much since he shifted to intelligence. Ribs assumed he would have updated his plans over the years, from a practical standpoint.

"I think everything's in place," Jordan said softly. "He's had those plans for so long, and somehow I never thought we'd use them."

"I know. The shock and pain are going to mix for a while. They'll probably take turns being more potent." For him the shock was winning. He knew Shimmer had been struggling with unseen ghosts for a while, and even so he couldn't believe he'd done it, couldn't believe he'd actually leave Jordan and the kids behind, to say nothing of all of them. A stab of anger tried to surface; he pushed it back down. *Later, there would be time to deal with his own stuff later. Right now it was about supporting Jordan.*

Nash finished nursing and lay in Jordan's lap, beaming up at them with a gummy smile. He had a few teeth now, but not all of them.

"He's so happy after he nurses," Jordan noted.

"Can't say that I blame him," Ribs said before he could even think about it.

Jordan's jaw dropped and her cheeks flushed. "Gaines, my lands."

"That came out wrong. What I meant was that obviously after he… With a full belly…There's really no way to rebound, huh?"

"'Fraid not, but it's okay. I mean I sort of did nurse him right in front of you, so that line probably got a little blurry. It's just that's kind of how I feel, a little blurry, like I'm trying to see and do everything through a thick wooly cloth right now. Sorry if that was awkward or uncomfortable." Her cheeks flushed again.

Ribs's arm was still around her. He used it to give her a reassuring squeeze. "Jordy, come on. It's part of life. I'm not one of those dinosaurs who thinks women and babies have to don a burqa to nurse. Babies get hungry, they eat. You're in your own house in your own bathroom. If anything I'm the intruder here."

"You could never be that," she said with her usual earnestness. "You're our family." Her smile dimmed. "My family, I guess. I mean I know you were Jay's first but..." she trailed helplessly away, as if realizing for the first time everything would need reassessed now.

"We're family, always and forever," he assured her, resting his head on hers. "And I am here for you, always, for anything you need. Call, and I will be here."

"I just...don't even know where to begin," she said, her gaze sliding around the bathroom as if only now realizing where she was, with no idea how she wound up there.

"Let's make our calls. I'll call Jay's parents. You call your mom."

"Right, okay," she said, reaching in her pocket for her phone. Ribs gave her shoulder a little squeeze as he reached for his own phone, then stood and walked out of the bathroom, perching on the edge of the bed.

Jordan started to cry almost immediately. The sound was distracting because it tugged something in him, something primal that needed to take action. He couldn't, though, not with his own call looming. So he turned his back toward the bathroom, squeezing his eyes closed until the moment Jay's mom answered the phone.

CHAPTER 6

Ribs intended to be there for Jordan as much as possible, but the next day her mother and Shimmer's parents arrived, setting up camp in her house and pushing out the friend group that longed to gather.

They met at Maggie and Ridge's instead, forming their own sort of wake for their friend, plotting ways to help and support Jordan moving forward. They'd been down this road before, unfortunately, too many times. Such was the world they inhabited that this would be the twelfth time Ribs acted as pallbearer for one of his former teammates or coworkers. This time felt different, however. Not only had Shimmer been his closest friend, but he was angry. Why hadn't Shimmer let him in, let him help? And how could he have left his family in the lurch this way? The selfish cruelty of his final act left him simmering, not to mention all the complex emotions where Jordan was concerned. He wanted to be there for her, to move in and set up camp to make certain she was okay and taken care of. And yet he had no right. She had no idea about his feelings for her and even if she did probably wouldn't return them. Her husband had just died, a man who had been both of their closest friend. The situation was rife with a mix of emotions, all of them bad. He felt grumpy, touchy, tense, like he wanted to cocoon himself away from everyone, including his friends.

But he didn't. Because he knew the temptation, because he understood where it could lead, he forced himself to reach out, to keep showing up, to keep talking and connecting so *he* didn't end up like Shimmer. It would be so easy to do, to begin to isolate himself, to listen to the voices in his head, to heed their lies. *No one cares, no one understands, no one will miss you when you're gone.*

Instead he called those lies out whenever they arose. He was surrounded by people who cared, by people who understood, by people who would miss him when he was gone.

Who depends on you, though?

That one was harder to answer. His work depended on him, but he was replaceable. The next SEAL or soldier was always waiting in the wings, ready to be a spy. Espionage was the world's oldest profession. As long as there were people, there would be spies.

Otherwise, what was his purpose? He had no wife, no children, not even a girlfriend.

The day of Shimmer's funeral arrived and Ribs didn't think he was the only one who didn't want to face it. All of them seemed to be dragging their feet, not making eye contact with each other as the funeral director gave them the rundown on what they needed to do with the casket. They were holding it together, but barely. For a group of former SEALs, keeping control of their emotions was mandatory. Except Jones who blubbered continuously, but no one minded because it was Jones; it would have been weird if he didn't cry.

The receiving line took place before the funeral. Maggie and Amelia were on Nash and Charlotte duty. Charlotte's stuffed dog had arrived. It was as big as she was, and she carried it everywhere, including to the funeral. The sight made Ribs smile, the only smile on such a grim day.

Jordan stood at the front of the room looking tired but pretty in her simple black dress. Amelia must have done her hair because it was softly curled and lay perfectly on her shoulders, making her look like the quintessential widow, blond and grave and feminine.

Ribs and the other guys hung back, letting the other friends and family snake through the line first. She held it together admirably until their group arrived and then she began to crack as first Ridge and then Ethan gave her a hug. By the time it was Ribs's turn, she was weeping and unable to support herself any longer. He led her to her seat and remained holding on, offering unspoken as well as actual physical support. Charlotte spied him and, connecting him with her beloved new dog, slid off her grandfather's lap and into his, snuggling into his embrace as best she could with her giant new dog between them. It helped to focus on her instead of his pain, so much that he almost felt bad for taking her from her grandparents. But soon they were enmeshed in their own grief, as was Jordan who shook with silent tears that ran unabated down her face. Ribs reached over and clasped her hand. She clung like a lifeline.

He had to let go when it was time to serve as pallbearer. He looked for a reasonable replacement to support her and found none. Her parents were both absorbed with their grief or with the children.

"Just hang on," Ribs murmured, giving her hand a squeeze before he had to let go. It felt like the motto for the entire day. *Just hang on and we'll somehow get through.*

The remainder of the day was interminable. In reality the processional and burial lasted the normal time. They only felt as though they stretched on for hours. By the end everyone was exhausted. This time the group didn't give Jordan up to her family; they all trekked back to her house where Amelia and Maggie had arranged for a post-funeral dessert buffet, which was a strange thing, unless anyone knew Amelia and Maggie and their legendary love of desserts. Somehow it helped to sit together and eat pie and cobbler and coffee.

Jordan fell asleep on the couch while everyone scurried around her, cleaning up, washing dishes, putting away toys, cuddling and loving on the kids. They said goodbye to Shimmer and Jordan's parents and left, one by one until only Ribs remained. He sat beside

Jordan on the couch, watching the steady rise and fall of her chest, willing her both to wake up and get some rest.

"She hasn't been sleeping," Jordan's mother confessed in a whisper, sitting in the chair beside the couch. Now both of them stared at Jordan as she continued to sleep. "Not just with this, but pretty much since Charlotte came along. I remember those days of having young babies, being so tired you can barely function. And now this. I worry. I've been trying to convince her to move back home where I can help."

Ribs worried, too, but Jordan moving away? Unthinkable. "What was her response to that?"

"She said it's too soon to make any decisions. She wants to let things settle before she figures out her next step. But she's so far from any family here." She shook her head sadly.

"She's not, though. We're all family here."

Her mom looked at him with a cross between amusement and pity. "I know you feel that way, and I know all you boys were close, being in the navy together and all. But it's not the same. Blood is thicker than water, as they say. Everyone has their own family, their own life to lead. After this initial hubbub, everyone will return to those lives and families, and then where will she be?" Once again she turned to stare at Jordan, this time worried.

Ribs stared at her again, too. It wasn't true, what her mother said. Maybe everyone else had families and lives to return to, but not him. He wouldn't be that guy who left Jordan and moved on when something shinier came along. "I don't have a wife or kids," he said. "They were mine by extension."

"I appreciate that, sweetie, and I know Jordan cares for you a great deal. You've been a good friend to them but, like him, your job takes you far away. He was gone so much, too much, and now…" She shook her head and faced Ribs. "Your job takes you away just as much and you don't live here. At least he was here part time, could add the salt to the softener and change the light bulbs. Now she'll have to do all that, too. If she moved home, all her family is there. Her uncles and cousins and brothers. We have a community, she'd be taken care of."

Her words made him squirm, mostly because they were true. He spent more than half his time traveling, like Shimmer. And unlike Shimmer he had his own house across town, one that was sadly neglected because he was also rarely there.

"We'll figure something out," he promised.

Jordan's mother pressed her lips together as if to say, *We'll see,* and both of them returned to staring at Jordan.

CHAPTER 7

For Jordan, being a mother meant she mostly no longer existed. Her life was about them now. Exercise consisted of those times she could stuff both kids into a stroller and jog until one or both of them began to fuss. She hadn't been to the dentist for a cleaning in three years. Her nails were broken to the nub and square on the ends because she had no time to file them. Makeup consisted of a moisturizing primer and tinted lip balm, and that was when she was feeling fancy. The only part of her that looked good was her hair, which Amelia had thankfully taken a personal interest in keeping alive. Her hair was colored and trimmed and styled and, in short, totally out of sync with the rest of her person.

She had no idea if this was how it was for all mothers or if it was because she was, in essence, a single mother while her husband spent so much of his life away. Or maybe she was simply bad at mothering. Maybe other women could nurse a baby all night and still make perfect little meals for their toddler that hit every nutritional high note while keeping themselves in shape, the house clean, the laundry done, and the yard weeded. Jordan couldn't. With the advent of her first child she went from a functioning working adult to a mombie, a woman who never got enough sleep and never seemed to be able to keep up with all the things she needed to do. And now she was a widow. But there was no time to mourn her husband or grieve the life they'd lost because she still needed to be a mom. So she kept going, putting one foot in front of the other moment by moment.

The first week after Jay's suicide was a blur of shock and trauma.

The second week, her mother and Jay's parents went home and life began to return to some semblance of normal. And there was a bit of comfort in the routine, of once again taking the kids to story time at the library and tucking them in for naps and middle of the night feedings for Nash. She had stopped trying to wean him because this was something tangible she could do for him, some comfort she could provide, even though he didn't know why he needed comfort.

Charlotte, who hadn't noticed Jay's absence, still somehow understood something was amiss. She had also been extra clingy and emotional the last couple of weeks. Jordan was glad, glad, glad for the stuffed dog Gaines bought her, the only highlight in a difficult time. She had named the dog "Wibs," in honor of Gaines, and he went with her everywhere—to bed, to the bathroom, in the car, and even to church. Someday maybe Jordan would consider getting them a real dog, but not now, not when she was still in survival mode.

Jay's death hurt her terribly. His suicide felt like a betrayal and condemnation. If only she had been there for him, been a better wife, maybe he wouldn't have taken his life. That was the lie she told herself when she was weak or tired. In her waking hours, she knew it wasn't true. He had struggled with things the last few years, things he couldn't talk about, things he had seen and done in his job and during his time as a SEAL. Each of his buddies had urged him to seek help, but he hadn't, wouldn't. His Mr. Tough Guy persona had been his downfall because he hadn't wanted to admit to any weakness, never realizing or believing that seeking the help he needed would have been the ultimate sign of strength.

Jordan was astute enough to realize it would take years to untangle all the complexity of his passing, not only for herself but for her kids. Someday she would have to explain to them Jay's absence and his decision to take his life. It was wholly unfair and she was mad. But she loved and missed him, too. All in all it was too much. It would be easy to sink under the weight of it, but her willful stubbornness wouldn't allow it. Someone had to parent her children and there was no one else to do it. And so she sucked it up and did what needed to be done, as she had been doing since she first married Jay and became a navy wife. In a way she had been practicing for widowhood her entire married life. Jay's long and many absences had felt like little deaths, especially after the kids came along. And in a way that she would never admit to anyone, it was a small relief to not be in between anymore. Being a single parent when Jay was away and then reorienting her entire life when he came home had been exhausting. She was sad and she was grieving, but at least it was finally settled: Jay was gone, fully and completely. Jordan was on her own. No one was coming to save her.

And so she rebounded better and faster than anyone expected. There was some comfort in surprising people with how well she was doing. She was keeping it together and keeping up with all that needed to be done, the way she always had. Life was moving on. The kids were in their routine, and so was Jordan. The house was messier than she wanted it to be, they relied on takeout more than they should have, but they were moving on.

Two weeks after Jay died, Jordan woke with a start, wondering if she heard Nash. She sat up. In the corner of her bedroom a man stared at her, unmoving and silent. Jordan froze, terrified, and then made herself speak.

"What do you want?"

He said nothing, did nothing, remained mute and motionless.

Could she reach for her phone? Would he attack? She risked it, slowly sliding her hand to the table beside her bed. She grabbed the phone, fingers shaking and numb with fear. It said a lot about her life that in that instant she decided to call one of her husband's friends instead of the police, but which one?

Gaines, obviously. He was the only one without a family to disturb. Her finger swiped his name until she remembered he was out of town on assignment—again, still, always.

"I'm calling 911," she told the person in the corner, hand still hovering over her phone. He remained still, unnaturally so. Emboldened or curious, she crept out of bed, easing closer until she could make out the form in the corner—the vacuum she'd left standing, along with a broom and a hoodie she'd carelessly tossed on top.

She remained blinking at it now, shock and embarrassment mingling. She had almost panicked and called the police on a mess of her own making. *Wow, Jordan. Wow.* In the beginning when she was newly married and Jay was deployed, she had been terrified this same way, had imagined the boogeyman behind every strange noise in the night. Eventually she grew used to being alone in the house. The paralyzing fear hadn't plagued her, but maybe the trauma had knocked it loose and reawakened it.

In the sink a dish clattered and she jumped, whirling in that direction with her hand on her heart.

You left dishes piled in the sink. One of them toppled, she coached herself. *This is an indictment against your housekeeping skills. If you hadn't left everything so messy, you wouldn't be having this problem.* She'd meant to clean the house today, she really had. But they'd had library day and Charlotte had dance class and then she had to run some errands, sign some legal papers with the bank. After trying to wrangle all the legalities of Jay's passing and then making supper and then urging the kids to eat supper, she had lacked the energy to vacuum and wash the dishes. Instead she'd dragged out the kids' tunnel, letting them zoom in and out and in and out, giggling, while she lay on the floor, letting the happy sounds of their laughter wash over her to try and erase some of the worst parts of the day.

She slipped back into bed and stared at the ceiling, not allowing her eyes to slide toward the empty space beside her. It wasn't as if Jay had filled it that often. He had been a part time husband, and she'd made her peace with that. If he had lived to retirement, they probably would have been one of those couples who had to learn to live together fulltime. And that was what hurt the most at the moment, knowing they would never get that chance. It wasn't the reality of what she'd lost right now that hurt so much because, in all honesty, it hadn't been that great. She and Jay had been fighting a lot. Jay was absent more than he was home. When he was home, he had been depressed and standoffish and also in denial about how depressed and standoffish he was.

But Jordan had maintained hope that it wouldn't always be that way. She'd been able to envision a future for them where they were back on track, back in love, getting along, able to laugh and love together. She'd pictured watching their kids grow up and sharing their milestones together—lost teeth, first days of school, graduation, marriage, becoming grandparents. Now all of that was lost. She would do those things by herself, and they would forever be tainted with the solemn realization that Jay had willingly taken himself out of the equation. It wasn't fair, it wasn't right, and it compounded her grief.

She was almost asleep again when she heard another dish tumble in the sink. Rolling her eyes at the mess, she reached for her phone and sent Gaines a text. One never knew where he was, which time zone he might be dealing with. Like Jay, she was used to the secrecy, had no real desire to know what he was doing or where. Sending a text to him now would be like firing into the void; maybe it would reach him, maybe it wouldn't. Maybe he didn't have his phone and wouldn't see it until he came back. In any case she should make it ambiguous enough to not worry him. She was a well-trained navy wife, after all. She knew the drill.

Please don't call the health department next time you see my house. The mess has become sentient.

To her surprise, he answered immediately. *No worries, I'm not a mandated reporter.*

I didn't wake you, did I? she asked, biting her lip. Knowing Gaines, he would answer her back even if it was the middle of the night where he was, if only to make certain she was okay. She had been counting on the fact that he wasn't available, otherwise she wouldn't have bugged him.

Nope. Sleep is for the weak.
Also the non-mothers.
Are you with Nash?

No. She paused, thinking. How much of her idiocy did she want to reveal? *I thought I heard him, but it wasn't. Just some dishes in the kitchen. Apparently I stink at dish Jenga.*

His answering text bubble appeared and disappeared a few times before he answered. *Are you sure it was only dishes? I could send Ridge or Ethan, if you're feeling uncertain.*

She pictured Maggie or Amelia having their husbands roused to come inspect her towering dish pile and cringed. *I'm sure. In case I didn't make it clear, the house is a disaster and is starting to complain. Really need to get it in gear and clean one of these days.*

Hire a maid.

I can't do that.

Why not?

Because I'm a stay at home mom.

So?

So we don't have maids. That's the point of being at home, so we can do all the things.

All the things are too much right now. Hire a maid and focus on yourself and the kids. No biggie.

She squinted, trying to see the mess through the darkness. How would she feel, hiring a maid to do the work she was supposed to be doing? *Could I actually do that?*

Yes, you have my permission, he replied.

I'll think about it.

Good. How are you, other than messy house that apparently talks?

I'm... She paused again. What could she say? Thriving? She wasn't. *Surviving.*

I'll be back in two days. Let's have supper. I'll pick something up.

I can cook, she insisted.

I know you can cook, but I don't want you to. Jordy, stop trying to do all the things, be all the things. It's okay to merely exist right now. Let us take care of you for a bit.

It doesn't come easily, she admitted.

For any of us, he agreed.

She thought that was probably true. None of the guys from their group of friends was the sort who accepted help easily or liked to depend on others. She didn't realize she felt the same until it happened to her. There was a sort of pride in being a competent Navy Wife. *I can survive my husband's long absences while holding down the fort at home. I can be ready to move on a moment's notice, sever all ties, and relocate on a whim. I can order my life around him and his schedule, always putting my needs and desires second. I can be an active member of the military community, caring for other spouses and families while their men are away.* Jordan had done it all, had dotted every i and crossed every t. And now that the shoe was on the other foot and she was failing, she realized how much unspoken pride she had taken in her position. Because now her pride was singed, her confidence dinged because, as it turned out, she couldn't do it all. Maybe she couldn't do any of it. She felt like she was floundering, sinking, and it was as terrifying as it was humbling.

What do you want for supper? Gaines asked, drawing her back to the present.

Surprise me, Jordan replied.

There's my adventurous girl, he said and Jordan felt her cheeks heat embarrassingly. He hadn't meant anything by the offhand comment, she knew. She wasn't his girl, and she was only moderately adventurous. But it had been a long time since anyone said anything remotely encouraging or endearing to Jordan. She was hungrier and needier than she realized, and she needed to be careful. The worst thing she could do during this difficult time would be to blunder into an inappropriate crush on one of Jay's friends. Gaines didn't see her that way, would never see her that way, and she wasn't at all ready for anything more than their long and casual friendship.

This time when she heard a sound, it was unmistakably Nash.

Gotta go, ask not for whom the baby wails; it wails for me, she sent.

Give the kiddos a kiss for me until I can do it in person. See you in two days.

See you, Jordan replied, setting her phone back on the stand, not allowing herself to acknowledge the flutter inside her, the one that looked forward to something for the first time in way too long. *I'm lonely,* she told herself, a situation that had been going on way before Jay passed. *I'm susceptible,* she also reminded herself, but then shook her head. If there was one person she didn't have to worry about, it was Gaines Hillcrest. He saw her as nothing more than a pesky little sister, she was certain. And that was how she would always remain, his best friend's wife who had somehow become a friend. They were pals, nothing more.

Nash wailed harder and with more urgency.

"Mama's coming," she said softly, shuddering when her voice disturbed the unnatural stillness of her bedroom.

CHAPTER 8

Ribs had to knock twice before Jordan answered the door. When she did so, it wasn't an exaggeration to say she looked like death warmed over, blond hair in a snarl, eyes puffy and red-rimmed, clothes sloppy and disheveled. She had an afghan wrapped around herself, and he didn't think she realized.

"Hey, sorry," she said, voice croaky with either missed or repressed sleep. She turned and stumbled away from him, back toward the couch where she collapsed in a heap.

"What's up?" he asked, dodging toys in his path until he reached the end of the couch and sat delicately by her feet.

"The kids are sick."

He sat up in alarm. "What? Are they okay? Do we need to take them to the doctor?"

She gave a sleepy chuckle. "No, they have sniffles. But sniffles upset them because they can't breathe and they haven't been sleeping. After only nursing at night the last couple of months, Nash now wants to nurse round the clock for comfort. I'm a little sleep deprived." As if to prove it, she closed her eyes.

"Where are they now?" He looked around. The house was silent.

"They were so fussy I thought I'd try to put them to bed and, miraculously, it worked. They both conked out almost immediately."

It was only a little after seven, which seemed early to him, but he knew nothing about children. Maybe it was a normal time. "I can go. You can sleep."

"Mmph," she said. He had no idea what that meant, but he took it to mean she wanted him to stay.

"Do you want to sleep first or eat first?" he picked up her foot, lying conveniently near his thigh, and rubbed his thumb in her instep.

She sat up, eyes wide with surprise.

He froze, somewhat abashed that he'd touched her so easily and without permission.

"That's, um, nice," she croaked.

He resumed his task, rubbing more of her foot, and she plopped backward onto the couch with a sigh, a contented one that time. "What was the question?"

"Sleep or eat?"

"It's hard to think when you're doing that," she noted, sounding dreamy.

He smiled. She was a mess and yet somehow completely adorable, especially with her face taking on that rapturous look. Jordan had always been ridiculously easy to please, he thought. She was low maintenance, unlike some women he'd dated who never seemed happy.

"When's the last time you ate?" he asked.

She squinted. "The kids' leftover oatmeal at breakfast?"

"Jordy," he intoned, giving her foot a squeeze.

Her eyes popped open. "What?" she asked, genuinely confused.

"You can't exist on leftover oatmeal."

She grinned. "You can, actually. You just end up looking like this." She held up a piece of her lank hair.

"Hey, new idea. You go shower."

She snorted a laugh.

"Not that I'm saying you need to. I merely meant you go take a few minutes for you while I set up supper." He squeezed her foot.

"That sounds amazing, but there's a tiny problem."

"What's that?"

"Now that I'm down, I don't think I have the energy to get back up again."

He leaned closer. "Want me to carry you?"

She jumped up and away. "Definitely no. You should not get close to this mother-of-preschooler stench I'm sporting. I'll be back. Eat without me if you're starved."

"I'll grab some leftover oatmeal if I can't take it," he assured her, smiling when she laughed.

While she was gone he picked up the toys from the floor and put them in the basket, then made his way to the kitchen and washed the towering stack of dishes. It was odd to see the house messy; every other time he'd been there it was spotlessly clean. He thought she was exaggerating about it being a mess until he saw it in person.

He was almost finished with the dishes when Jordan stood at the edge of the room behind him and gasped. "Gaines, you did the dishes? You're the best."

"Hey, my mom was a nurse who worked a ton. Her motto was 'help out or starve and go naked.' No free rides in my house."

"I love that," Jordan said cheerfully. She made her way into the room, pausing to pick up toys from the floor around the high chair. "But I have to say that if I took a picture of you right now, I could probably sell it for lots of money. There has to be some website some-where titled SEALs Doing Dishes or something."

"If you find it, please never let me know," he said. She deposited a load of items on the counter. He finally looked at her and stopped short, mouth gaping. Her hair was wet and piled on top of her head in some kind of loose bun, and she wore a robe. That robe did things to him, short circuiting his brain until all he could do was wonder what she was wearing beneath it.

"I can't tell you the last time I had an unaccompanied shower. I usually plug the bath and let the kids play in the overflow, then rinse them when I'm done like puppies. This was so great. Thank you." She eased to his right and gave him a side hug.

"Oh, that's, sure…" he mumbled, awkward now in the extreme as he debated leaving his hands in the water or using them to draw her into a real hug. The real hug scared him because he didn't think he'd be able to control it. So he remained half wet and bumbling like he was twelve and noticing girls for the first time.

"Why don't you leave the rest of those, friend. Let's eat." She tugged his sleeve and turned toward the bag of food he'd brought.

He was thankful for the reprieve, for a concrete place to turn his mind. "I got a little extra because I thought the kids would be eating with us. I didn't think about the time, sorry."

"It's fine. They eat early, like we're living in a retirement home or something. Early bird specials were made for people like us." She tossed him a smile and returned her attention to removing food from the bag, a good thing since the smile short circuited his brain again. She was clean and fresh and warm and good smelling and she was *wearing a robe.* Were there clothes beneath the robe? Was she purposely trying to kill him or did she really not think how the robe would affect him, all white and fluffy and soft and intriguing? Jordan wasn't the type of woman who played games or toyed with people, but how could she earnestly not know how appealing that was? Especially when she sat and the robe slipped and he caught a tantalizing preview of leg and thigh before she pulled it closed again. *So this is what it feels like when a brain melts,* he thought, staring hard at the sandwich she'd set in front of him.

"This looks and smells amazing," she murmured, inhaling deeply.

Yes it does, he agreed, eyes darting to her face in time to see her close her eyes and smile. She opened them, caught him staring, and froze.

"You're making fun of me," she accused.

"Really, really no. Why would I make fun of you?"

"Because I'm having this overt reaction to food and dishes," she motioned helplessly toward the sink. "I'm usually the one who's doing all the things, making the food and cleaning, and it's so, *so* nice to have a night off. Thank you."

She beamed at him and he felt like his heart might actually explode from the combined pain and joy of it. "You're welcome." Their eyes caught and held and he thought maybe he wasn't the only one who felt a little off kilter when she dropped hers and picked up her sandwich.

"My mom's been beating the drum relentlessly, trying to get me to move home."

"I thought you weren't going to make any decisions for a year," he reminded her, tamping down his sudden panic. Jordan moving away? Unthinkable.

"That's the line I keep spouting, but I wonder why? What's the point of waiting when it's what I'll probably end up doing anyway."

"What? Why? Why would you do that?"

"I'm kind of all alone here, Gaines."

"Uh, hello," he pointed to himself.

She smiled. "You're sweet, and you're a pal, but you have your own life. Everyone does. Amelia helps out when she can, but she's so busy. You work a crazy amount and someday…"

"Someday what?" he asked when she trailed off.

"Someday you'll have a family of your own, as you should. I need to figure out a permanent solution for us. The kids would have cousins, if I moved home."

"And what about you? What would you have?"

"Someone to call, in case of emergency," she said.

"You have that here," he said, pointing to himself again, this time with more urgency.

She gave him the smile again and shook her head. "I don't, though. You're gone more than you're here, like Jay. It's weird because he was gone so much I learned to adapt. But now that he's *gone* gone, I feel so…vulnerable." She shuddered and drew the robe tighter.

"Jordy, I hate this. I don't want you to feel like you can't count on me."

"It is what it is, Gaines." She paused and bit her lip. "Can I give you a piece of unsolicited advice?"

He nodded.

"When you find that girl, that special someone, make sure she knows in advance what she's in for, that she's well suited. The long and frequent absences, they take a toll. Before we had kids, it was fine, almost fun. Not that I didn't miss Jay, but it was an excuse to go out with my girlfriends or stay in and read a book, do a manicure, watch a movie. But then after kids…I feel like a bomb went off, like someone took a wrecking ball to everything that was. I had no idea single parenting would be this hard. So just…just make sure she has informed consent, okay? Save yourself a whole lot of drama and heartache." She reached across the table and squeezed his forearm.

He shifted his arm and grasped her hand again. "I'm sorry, Jordy, that it was so hard before, and that it continues to be hard now."

"It's going to get better, I know. I can almost see it, almost feel it. This season of no sleep and no time will be gone, and I'll miss it. Or at least that's what people so helpfully tell me when Nash is having a full on meltdown in the grocery store." She rolled her eyes.

"Let me ask you this: if you felt like you had a better support system here, would you still want to go back to your family?"

She snorted. "No. My mom about had a cow when I married Jay, as I'm sure you remember, but even as a twenty year old child bride I knew it was the right thing to do, and I knew I needed that buffer between myself and my family who never had an opinion on my life they didn't care to express. I love them, but they drive me insane. Moving there would be for the kids, not for myself."

"Then please, please stick with the original plan. Give it a year and make certain it's the right thing, okay?"

"I can't imagine what difference a year will make," Jordan replied. She studied him through narrowed eyes, probably trying to figure out his angle or vested interest in keeping her there.

"Please? For me? I…I don't want you to go. I don't think I could take it."

"Hey," she said softly, giving his hand a squeeze. "You'll always be involved in our lives, okay? The kids will want to know their dad's best friend. You have all the good stories they'll someday want to hear."

"It's…not…just…the…kids," he choked.

"I know," Jordan said, tone sympathetic.

"You do?" he asked, breath and heart temporarily stopped.

"Yes, it was hard, losing him like that. Maybe you and the other guys feel a little survivor's guilt because, with all you went through together, he's the one that chose to end it. But you tried, Gaines. I heard you try, so many times to reach him and help. And I appreciate it, more than you know. It means the world to me that you tried that hard. His mind wasn't right the last couple of years." She paused and brushed her eyes. "He couldn't see a better time, couldn't see the other side when we'd work our way through the hurt. But it's not your fault, and it would kill me if you felt in any way like it was."

He did feel some guilt over Shimmer's suicide, was plagued by all the *if onlys*. If only he'd tried harder, if only he'd dragged him to some kind of therapy or intervention or PTSD treatment. But that wasn't what he meant. He meant he couldn't lose her, didn't know how he'd survive if she packed up and moved away. It would feel like his heart packed up and went with her. And she had no idea. And her husband, his best friend, had only been gone two weeks. *What is wrong with me?*

He had no idea, and he wouldn't find an answer tonight. So he let her believe it was about Shimmer and not about her. But he couldn't stop himself from reaching for her, from pulling her into an enveloping hug. *Friends can hug*, he assured himself.

Jordan seemingly saw nothing amiss in the action. She snuggled into his embrace, wrapping her arms around him, going all in on it like he somehow knew she would. Before, when Shimmer was alive, he'd only given her cursory hugs, a light embrace on her wedding day, to say goodbye at the end of a visit or thank her for a good meal. This was something different, something possessive that reflected all he currently felt. Maybe it was wishful thinking on his part, but he thought it was what Shimmer would have wanted. *Take care of her.* He would do that in the best way he knew how, as soon as he figured out exactly what that was.

CHAPTER 9

"How are you?"

When the question was asked by your former team leader, a man who was working his ranks to the higher realms of the intelligence community, it had more significance than a casual, "What's up?"

Cameron Ridge sat behind his massive wooden desk, squinting at Ribs in concern as he awaited his answer, reading between the lines as ever.

"I'm all kinds of things," Ribs answered honestly.

"What's winning?" Ridge asked.

"Anger. And fear."

"The anger I get, but why the fear?" Ridge asked.

Ribs picked up a paperweight, started to toy with it, saw Ridge eyeing him in disapproval, and set it back down. Like The Colonel, Ridge had a low tolerance for fidgeting. "Jordan's talking about moving away, closer to home."

Ridge blinked at him. "Maybe that's for the best."

"What?" Ribs exclaimed. "Of course it's not. She can't go."

"I meant maybe it's what's best for Jordan, not for you. Think about it from her point of view."

Ribs stubbornly shook his head.

Ridge expelled a breath, annoyed or impatient, it was hard to tell. "Look, I am telling you as a dad, having family around is important. I never thought I would be happy to have Darren nearby, but he picks up the baby and watches him for two hours every Wednesday until Maggie gets off work. And Amelia is our backup whenever we're stuck. You don't realize how invaluable your family is until you become a parent. We literally couldn't make it without them some days."

"I could be her support," Ribs insisted.

Ridge tipped his head at him. "When you're in town, you mean, and not working twenty hours a day on a case."

Ribs's mouth opened to argue, but no sound came out. Instead he sat back, deflated. "She can't go. She can't. I cannot take losing her, too."

"Does she know?"

"No." Ribs gave a rueful chuckle and swiped his hand over his face. "I don't think she'd realize if I hired a skywriter."

"Women," Ridge agreed, shaking his head. "I had to spell it out for Maggie. She had no idea."

"What? Everyone knew," Ribs said.

"Not Maggie. But back to you. Here's what I'm saying, suppose you make it clear to Jordan, then what?"

"Then we live happily ever after?" Ribs said hopefully.

Ridge rolled his eyes. "What can you offer her that she doesn't already have? She's going to have Shimmer's insurance, so she's financially set. She's used to being on her own and still would be. What, exactly, would you add to her life?"

"This isn't exactly the encouraging pep talk I hoped for," Ribs admitted.

"Then make it so. Fix what needs to be fixed, then get your girl."

"Right," Ribs nodded. "So we're both clear, what needs to be fixed?"

Ridge took that breath he took whenever it was clear he was dealing with an idiot. He rested his hands on the desk and leaned forward. "Losing Shimmer was a trauma. Losing him that way was worse. But before that, Jordan had been dealing with a lot, mostly his absenteeism. Single parenting has taken a toll. What would be different about you in that scenario?"

"Are you saying I should quit my job?" Ribs snorted.

Ridge spread his hands imploringly and shrugged.

Ribs sat up, now truly alarmed. "I can't quit my job. I love my job."

"Then I guess you need to choose. Because I am telling you as a friend to you both, as well as a husband and a father, that you cannot have both right now, not at this time, not with this woman. She's way too fragile to take on another ex-SEAL turned spy."

Ribs stared at his former commander, openmouthed and blinking. Never in all his life did he believe he would hear Cameron Ridge telling him to quit his high profile, hard-earned, espionage job for a woman.

"What would I even do?" he asked.

Ridge shrugged again. "That's for you to figure out. Jones made it work."

Ribs grimaced. They had all given Jones a hard time when he chose the soft life over continuing to do field work or remain in the navy. On the other hand, Jones had someone now. They were planning a future together, saving for their eventual retirement and children. He would be a fulltime, hands-on dad. For the first time in his life, Ribs began to envy that, to envy *Jones*. "Oh, geez," he muttered, shaking his head.

Ridge smiled as if he could read his thoughts, which he probably could. "Let me tell you this: I dreaded leaving the field to take a supervisory roll, thought I would hate every bureaucratic moment of it. But it's still challenging, still exciting. Maybe not in the same way, but I haven't turned into the brain dead, atrophied zombie I feared. I'm still working hard, still fulfilled. I look forward to each day, maybe even a little more now because, statistically speaking, my chances of coming home alive are much higher."

"I'll keep an open mind," Ribs promised. It was the best he could do. Right now he felt torn because the thought of leaving his beloved job felt as bad as the thought of losing Jordan. At this point there wasn't a clear winner in his mind. But maybe if he had somewhere else to go, something else to do, a way to imagine a life outside the one he currently lived, maybe then he'd be able to let go and move on.

"One final word and I'll drop it. As a boss, I am telling you this: if you die on the job, people will be sad, but I'll have your replacement waiting in the wings and ready to go in five minutes. If you die as a husband and father, you'll leave a hole forever."

Ridge always had a way of making him think about things, deep things he would otherwise prefer not to ponder. Even though he was only a few years older, he had that type of wisdom Ribs thought could only be gained by life in the country or, in Ridge's case, on a sprawling ranch in the middle of Texas. *Ranch Wisdom*, the guys used to call it, back in the day whenever Ridge turned philosophical. Back then, when action had been their bread and butter, it hadn't happened so often. Now they all sort of depended on it. Despite the fact that they hadn't been SEALs for half a decade, he would forever be their leader.

"Thanks," he said sincerely.

"We're all rooting for you. For both of you," Ridge said.

"You've turned sentimental," Ribs accused.

"Marry an amazing woman, have a beautiful baby, and see if it doesn't happen to you, too," Ridge said.

Ribs didn't reply because, from where he was sitting, it sounded ideal.

⚷

This time Jordan was ready. She was showered and wearing clothes, hard pants and not her usual yoga wear (despite the fact that she hadn't done yoga since her twenties, she somehow had an entire wardrobe of yoga attire.) The house, while not immaculate, was at least tidy, and she had made supper. Meatloaf, Gaines's favorite.

He was right on time as usual. Navy life wasn't really conducive to people who couldn't keep to a schedule. So much training over so many years had a way of beating the undisciplined portions out of a man. All of the guys were generally early for everything, except Jones who tended to be the most scattered. He rang the bell, which struck Jordan as odd. It was much too formal for their long acquaintance.

She opened the door and saw greenery.

"I bought you a plant," he announced cheerfully, holding it aloft.

"Oh," Jordan said, trying not to cringe. A plant would be one more thing that depended on her, one more thing to try and keep alive.

"It's fake," he added in a whispered aside.

She laughed and reached for it. "You do know me."

"Yep," he agreed, and then he leaned in. And kissed. Her cheek. Jordan froze like the proverbial deer, unaccustomed to the new ritual. Was this a thing they did now? Should she kiss his raspy, good smelling cheek in return? Thinking of his smell caused her to inhale deeply.

"Are you sick?" he asked, taking a step back as his eyes swept over her in concern.

"In the head, maybe," she said. *Get it together. You've smelled men before. Four weeks as a widow and you've become a walking hormone.*

"Join the club," he said, closing the door. She noted that he took a look around outside before he did so, a thing Jay had also done. It was as if they couldn't stop being alert, looking for trouble, scanning for hotspots. Jordan had always liked it, enjoyed the feeling of safety and protection it provided. It highlighted a gnawing underlying feeling of insecurity since Jay's passing. *I will probably never have that again,* she thought. Those random and depressing thoughts had been happening more often, as if now that the shock was wearing off the reality of grief began its dark descent. Jordan would probably never sleep next to a solid, reliable man again, never be held in his arms, soothed, kept safe from all life's terrors. Even though Jay was gone a lot, she had taken his alpha-male status for granted, always knowing she was well protected in his presence. Being without that now left a gaping hole of low-level anxiety.

"You got awfully silent," Gaines said, reaching out to squeeze her shoulder.

"Sorry, I didn't sleep great."

"Nash?" he guessed.

"No, my imagination. I keep…" she broke off, embarrassed.

"Keep what?"

"I keep hearing things. House noises I never noticed before, which is completely ridiculous because we've lived here four years and I spend many of those nights here alone. But everything feels different now. Dumb, I know."

"Hey, not dumb. Not dumb at all. You're going through a monumental life shift right now. Lean into it, don't back away and try to talk yourself out of it. It's okay to feel…"

"All over the place and completely mixed up?" she volunteered.

"Yes," he agreed. "You're allowed to feel exactly how you feel, at any given moment. No apologies." He clasped her hand and gave it a squeeze.

Jordan stood there, staring at him, a little bit dazed, unable to put a name to the newness. Their still-clasped hands swung idly between them. Gaines smiled. She smiled in return. The moment felt like it was about to stretch into something more, and then Charlotte barreled into him, wrapping her dog-laden arms around his legs while Nash squealed and tossed his cup from his high chair.

And we're back, Jordan thought with a little bit of relief. Whatever was going on, she was certain it was completely one sided and due to her rattled, sleepless state. Gaines only saw her as a pal, his best friend's girl, more like a sister than anything else. That was how it had always been between them, how it would always be. She was not nor never had been on his level, which was perfectly okay because they were friends. Friends-in-law, really. Their mutual love for Jay had been their deepest connection.

"Uncle Wibs," Charlotte declared. Since the arrival of her stuffed dog, he had been her favorite person, which was an unmitigated relief because it offered a distraction from Jay's absence. The kids were used to not seeing him—Charlotte still hadn't asked where he was. But someday Jordan would have to explain in a way she could understand. She was dreading that day.

"Baby girl," Gaines declared, picking up Charlotte and tossing her in the air before kissing both cheeks. Like most women in the direct glare of his focus, Charlotte squealed and blushed with delight. Even little girls seemed to understand and appreciate Gaines's uncommon beauty and perfection. The man was an Adonis.

Once again Jordan realized she was staring at him, having thoughts, and made herself snap into focus. What on earth was wrong with her? She'd known him for more than a decade and never suffered more than a detached sort of recognition of his good looks, the same way she could appreciate Ethan and Ridge's beauty. They were devilishly handsome men; such was life. Jordan had always been much more comfortable with everymen like Jay and Jones, attainable men who didn't make you feel aware of every flaw within yourself. Even now she patted her hair, attempting to right all that had gone wrong since Amelia last laid hands on her.

"We're having meatwoaf," Charlotte told Gaines importantly. "Cause Mommy said it's your favorite."

"Did you know the first day I met your mom, she served me meatloaf?" Gaines said.

"I did?" Jordan asked, tossing him a smile. "How on earth do you remember what you ate, after all these years?"

"It was a momentous day," he said.

Jordan pressed her lips together and turned toward the stove. What did that mean? *He must have received some kind of award or commendation that day and I've forgotten,* she assured herself, certain that meeting her and eating meatloaf hadn't ranked high enough on his life events to be termed "momentous."

"Hey, buddy," Gaines said, pausing to bend over and kiss the top of Nash's head. Jordan's heart melted a little. What was it about tough guys and babies that did that? So strong, yet so tender and gentle. It was likely Gaines had personally killed a few people, and yet he stood in her kitchen, loving on her kids.

Jay had been the same for a while, but the disparity had started to wage war in his mind. He seemed unable to resolve the things he'd seen and done with who he wanted to be, began having terrible nightmares, lashing out at Jordan and even sometimes the kids. He hadn't become violent with them, but there were times when his temper made him unrecognizable to her, she who believed she knew him so well.

"Can I help?" Gaines asked, coming alongside her and squeezing her shoulder again. She stared up at him with big eyes, taking a moment to disconnect from her memories. Would the same thing that happened to Jay someday happen to Gaines? Were all of them doomed by their difficult and burdensome jobs?

"Jordy," Gaines prompted, smoothing his thumb along her neck.

"Do you ever worry about it?" she whispered, pausing to lick her dry lips. "Ending up like Jay?"

"I'd be lying if I said I didn't, but Jay and I were different. His family dynamic was such that…" he glanced at Charlotte, not wanting to say too much. "He was more old school. My mom was pretty good about getting us to open up, making us connect, identify, and talk about our feelings. My dad was a hugger, a bawler, was tender and connected to his soft side. I guess I don't really have much trouble telling people when I'm sinking, never really had that macho urge to try and heal myself. If I'm in trouble, you better believe I'm going to be the first in line to get help."

She thought that was probably true, especially after hearing him urge Jay so many times over the years to get help. His thumb was still smoothing along her neck, and it felt so good. The lack of touch the last few weeks made the touch almost feel like sensory overload now. "Gaines," Jordan whispered.

"Yes," he whispered in return, staring at her lips when she licked them again. The baby ate her lip balm, and she desperately needed more. He was probably noting how dry and cracked her lips were, and she fought a cringe.

"Charlotte's birthday is in a couple of weeks and we're having a party. I hope you can make it."

"Pwease," Charlotte chimed in, giving his neck a crushing squeeze. "Pwease, Uncle Wibs."

"I'll try," he said, hating that it was the best he could do. He had no idea where he'd be two days from now, let alone two weeks. "I'll try," he added again, this time to Jordan.

She smiled, but he thought it looked sad. Or maybe resigned. She more than anyone knew it would be useless to give a promise he might not be able to keep. Suddenly Ridge's words of wisdom made sense because if anyone deserved someone to keep his word and be there, it was Jordan. The fact that he couldn't provide that when she needed it most kind of killed him. But what could he do? What was the answer? He had no idea and a great sense of urgency to find it.

CHAPTER 10

Finding mom friends was like dating, only worse. At least men put off understandable signals, either "I'm interested" or "back off." With women there were so many variables. *Do I like you, do you like me, do our values line up, will you judge my messy house and daughter's snarled hair, do our children get along, is your kid a bully, are you that mom who makes her baby learn Mandarin to get a leg up,* and on and on it went. Jordan had lived in DC for four years and been unable to break in anywhere, despite trying library time, a tumble class, and mommy and me pottery. (That one was a complete disaster. Between trying to keep Nash out of clay and realizing she had zero latent talent as a sculptor, her so-called mug had ended up like an anatomically correct heart with a handle.)

It was another gut punch to her self-esteem in what had already been a rough few years. Becoming a mother, losing her figure, losing sleep, feeling like she was failing at everything, having another baby in the midst of that chaos, trying to navigate it all alone while her husband traveled incessantly. On top of that the rejection from other moms felt like too much. If she had to be perpetually pudgy and exhausted now, at least she could have had a friend to aid the journey.

Amelia was a friend, but she wasn't a mother and she was perfect, so it was hard to relate.

But today at last she had been invited to a play date. After edging closer and closer to the moms at library story time, trying to project openness without being needy, she had finally been granted entrée into their group.

"We're all going to my house to hang out for a bit. Want to come?" One of the moms named Nee said.

"Sure, yes, okay," Jordan said, nodding like a bobble head. *Stop nodding, stupid,* she urged herself. "Can I bring anything?"

"No, I think we're good. I made some gluten free seaweed bites," Nee said.

Jordan almost laughed because she thought it was a joke. Thankfully she refrained. That should have been the first clue she was in trouble, but she blundered ahead, desperate to make contact with the outside world.

She followed Nee to her home in a normal looking neighborhood, only a few blocks from her own. But that was where the similarities ended. At the end of the driveway, for instance, was a sign proclaiming that they were a "chemical-free" home and did not allow the city to spray near their property.

The city sprays our properties? Why? What for? Jordan thought. Was she supposed to be concerned about that? She added it to the overflowing list of things she was supposed to worry about, but it tumbled so far to the bottom it would likely be forgotten soon.

She unbuckled the kids, whispering to Charlotte to have good manners, and approached the door. And saw her worst nightmare—white carpet. With sudden panic she glanced at Charlotte's shoes, a clump of dirt jumping out at her. Of course they would have to go to a house with white carpet on a day they went to the muddy park. As soon as they were inside, she set Nash down and took off Charlotte's shoes, noting with further dismay that her left sock had a giant hole in the toe.

By the time she was finished with Charlotte's shoes, Nash had crawled away and directly to a glass-fronted curio cabinet. With horror, she saw him reach his sticky paws toward the glass and leapt, nearly diving on top of him in her haste to swoop him up and rescue the pristine glass.

When she stood upright, Nee was watching her, smile plastered on her face. Perhaps that was the moment they both realized this was a gross mismatch, but it would only go downhill from there.

"How are you coming with your preschool applications?" Nee asked as she led Jordan's trio down the hall to the playroom. They arrived in the door and Jordan stopped short because it was like a playroom from a magazine, filled with modernist wooden toys that looked like they had been crafted by Dutch gnomes with doctorates in child development.

"This is so nice," Jordan blurted, gaping in the doorway.

"Thank you," Nee said absently, probably not understanding Jordan's awe. At their house somehow the entire place had become one giant playroom with toys strewn haphazardly, some in the kitchen, some in the family room. Recently some had even made their way to Jordan's bedroom so the kids would be occupied while she attempted to fold laundry. But outside of this room, it was as if children didn't live here. And while her children immediately headed toward bins and began tossing things asunder, Nee's child sat at a table, placidly working on something that was probably STEM approved and brain enhancing.

Once the kids were safely secured in the room (using a state of the art gate that had an electronic alert system and camera Nee could monitor from her phone), Jordan finally returned to the hovering question.

"To be honest, I haven't even looked at preschool. I should probably do that." Her fingers twisted anxiously. She actually had intended to start scouring for preschools, but Jay's death preempted everything else for a while.

"Oh," Nee said, stopping short. "I hope you get in."

"Did you get in somewhere?" Jordan asked, already knowing the answer.

"Oh, yes. We applied as soon as Clipper was born. He's going to Ravenswood."

"Oh, that sounds nice," Jordan said. What she was really thinking was *how did I not know her kid's name was Clipper?*

"It's a little over our budget, but it's the foundation for everything, you know? That's why we started saving before we even had kids."

"For preschool," Jordan clarified.

"Oh, yeah," Nee said, nodding. "Without the right preschool, kids can't get in to the right elementary school."

"Doesn't that just depend on which district you live in?" Jordan asked.

Nee laughed hard. "Good one. Obviously the only way we would send him to public school would be with a personal tutor and armed guard."

"Yeah," Jordan said weakly. Were the public schools that bad? One of the reasons she and Jay had chosen their particular suburb was because of the well-manicured elementary school a few blocks away. She had envisioned the time when she would walk her kids to and from school each day, safely tucking them in the care of teachers who would educate them. But if what Nee said was true, that was the equivalent of sending them to prison without any gum or cigarettes to use as currency.

"Are you vegan?" Nee asked as they reached the kitchen.

"I...no," Jordan said slowly. Was she supposed to be? Would it be one more thing she was doing wrong in their eyes?

"Me neither," Nee said. Jordan's sigh of relief was short lived when she continued. "We eat traditional, Paleo, you know?"

No, Jordan did not know. She had no idea. To her it was a victory if she got her kids to eat a vegetable a day.

"Help yourself to pâté," Nee said. And then she motioned to a spread on the kitchen counter that looked like the White House chef stopped by and set up camp for a bit. Jordan had never seen a canapé in real life before, but she was certain she saw some now as trays were lined with little tiny swirls of vegetables in various artistic arrangements.

"Did you have this catered?" Jordan blurted. In her mind there was no other possible explanation, unless she'd bought a tray from Costco and unloaded it onto her own platters.

Nee laughed again as if Jordan had made a funny joke. Again. "Nah, I like to keep healthy snacks in the fridge at all times."

Jordan thought of her fridge, currently loaded with leftover meatloaf and half a pizza. "Yes, right, exactly." Absently she reached for a cracker, one shaped like a star, and spread it with the pâté. It was sort of salty, sort of rich, kind of amazing actually.

"This is the only way I can get my kids to eat liver," Nee confessed, as if it was a dirty secret.

Jordan froze, mouth filling with saliva as the actual meaning of pâté became clear. Liver. *Liver.* Not cheese, like she vaguely thought. Fighting her gag reflex, she made herself swallow. The doorbell rang and Nee excused herself to answer. Jordan grabbed a glass bottle of water—*a glass bottle*—and guzzled a few sips. The liver hadn't tasted bad, not at all. *But it was liver.* She needed to tell someone immediately to reaffirm that she was not insane.

Accidentally ate liver, she sent Gaines.

He replied a minute later. *Some sort of ritual? Hopefully not from a live donor. Blink once if you're part of a cult now.*

Nee returned, along with a few other women, and Jordan stuffed her phone away, pasting on a smile. They were all the same, she suddenly realized, artfully coiffed hair and makeup, matching messy buns and expensive hiking clothes. They were somehow already involved in a conversation about Ravenswood, the special preschool their children had already been accepted to.

"Oh, pâté. Yours is the best, Nee," one of them said, eagerly reaching for the pâté knife.

Surreptitiously Jordan reached for her phone and sent Gaines a text. *Blink.*

*N*ot surprisingly the day went downhill from there. Jordan might have been able to blend into the woodwork except conversation turned to Jay.

"What does your husband do?" one of the women, Janelle, asked. Jordan felt like the women held their collective breath, waiting to pass judgment in case Jay did something blue collar for a living.

"Oh, actually my husband died," she said. It was the first time she'd had to tell anyone, and it was harder than she'd thought it would be. And it went over even worse, settling like a lead balloon, bringing down the energy of the room until all conversation died and everyone was staring at her.

"Oh," Nee said, pressing her hand to her heart. "I am so sorry. I had no idea. How long has he been gone?"

Jordan cleared her throat. "Four weeks."

Somehow, impossibly, the silence deepened. Maybe she was being overly sensitive, but it was as if she could feel their judgment. *Her husband only died four weeks ago and she's out? She's going to story time and play dates?*

"How did he die?" a woman named Marie asked. The other women shot her death looks, but Jordan didn't mind. Theoretically at least.

But then she said, "Suicide," and mouths dropped. If there were any pearls in the room, they'd be clutched right now. The silence was so intense it was hard to breathe. Tears pricked behind Jordan's eyes. This was her first real attempt at an outing since Jay's passing, and it was going even worse than she'd imagined.

"Well," Nee said, clapping her hands together to get everyone's attention. It was so silent that all the women jumped, startled. "Should we feed the kiddos? No one's allergic to macadamia, are they?"

One woman raised her hand. "Blarney is allergic to all tree nuts."

Jordan coughed hard and everyone turned to look at her. She pointed to her throat, "Cracker," she croaked, a total lie because she hadn't eaten anything since the pâté debacle. But come on. *Blarney.* Who names their child after a mythic Irish stone? She guzzled water and followed behind the other moms to retrieve her children, counting the moments until she could make her escape.

Never leaving home again, she thought now as she lay in bed, cozy and warm and relaxed. What was so bad about being a hermit, really? The advent of delivery had made it so convenient to never have to deal with outsiders. So her children would be weird and standoffish, and probably stupid and malnourished if today was any indication. At least they weren't named Clipper or Blarney.

That was her last thought before she drifted to sleep. An unknown time later, she startled awake. *Nash?* She lay perfectly still, willing both of them to go back to sleep. Sometimes if she ignored him a few minutes he settled down. Other times he got worked up and only nursing him would do. She rolled onto her back in order to hear better, and that was when she saw him, the man standing in the corner watching her.

This time she sighed. *Why did I leave the vacuum out again?*

But that thought was immediately followed by, *I didn't.* She had put the vacuum away before Gaines arrived, she made certain because she wanted everything to be clean. She stared at the spot, trying to figure out what this new apparition might be, but instead of standing still like last time, the figure moved and walked out of the room.

Jordan sat up, heart hammering so hard it whooshed blood through her ears, obscuring all other sound. Hands shaking, she reached for her phone and pushed the emergency call button, too flustered to think what else to do.

"911, what is your emergency?"

"There's someone in my house," Jordan whispered, hating the way her voice shook, her hands shook, her everything shook. Her husband had been a Navy SEAL. Why had zero percent of his bravery rubbed off on her?

And then all at once she remembered the kids. What if the man left her room to get to one of them? She was out of bed and sprinting down the hall before she even gave the dispatcher her address.

Both the kids' doors were open, she noted in some part of her brain. She always closed them at night, always, especially after that terrifying fire safety video she watched about how much closing doors slows the progression of a house fire.

If he hurt my kids... The thought trailed away because she didn't know how to finish it, except that she would find a way.

Her eyes went first to the kids, still sleeping in their beds, before trailing slowly around their rooms, making certain no one was there. It was probably the wrong way to do things. She had vague memories of Jay telling her you had to neutralize the threat before you took care of any victims, but whoever wrote that rule obviously hadn't been a mother. Once her kids were okay, she could relax.

"Ma'am? *Ma'am,*" the dispatcher said. Her growing urgency told Jordan she had probably been trying to get her to respond for some time.

"Sorry," Jordan whispered, sliding to a crouch in the hallway. "I was checking on my kids. They're fine and he wasn't in either of their rooms."

"Where are you now?"

"I'm in the hallway." She paused and listened. "I don't hear anything. Maybe he's gone?"

"The officers will be there soon. I'll stay on the line with you until they arrive. Tell me if anything changes."

"Okay," Jordan said, taking a deep breath, her first, since she was jolted awake. She worked on bringing her heart rate out of the stratosphere.

"Is there anyone you can call to come be with you?" the dispatcher asked.

"Yes," Jordan said. "But I'll have to wait until we disconnect."

"Okay, just keep the officers informed of his arrival. The first unit is arriving on the scene. Please proceed to the front door and open it slowly."

"Okay," Jordan replied, suppressing a semi-hysterical bubble of laughter. She appreciated the dispatcher's help and reassurance, but who talked that way in real life? *Unit, proceed.* It would have seemed more natural if she said, "Girl, the police are here. Get up out of that crouch and open the door." Or maybe not. Maybe Jordan wouldn't have felt as secure if she talked like a real person instead of a humanoid robot.

Cautiously, Jordan opened the door. Two officers stood on the other side, reminding her so much of Jay it felt like a sucker punch. Not that they looked like him. One of them was black, in fact. But it was that air they had, the authoritative I'm-here-to-help-and-possibly-lower-the-boom expression. And the stance. She'd missed the stance, so much a part of Jay he couldn't seem to turn it off, even when he was at home. Her eyes flooded with tears that overflowed and ran down her cheeks.

"Ma'am?" one of them said, posture relaxing slightly. "Are you okay?"

"Yes, I...Sorry. Please come in." She moved aside and ushered them in.

"Did I hear you unlock this door before you opened it?" one of them asked.

"Yes. It was locked," she said, frowning as his meaning became clear. If the door was locked, it meant the intruder either got out another way or was still in the house.

Tense and alert once more, the officers put their hands on their guns. "We're going to need you to stay put while we search the premises."

Premises. Call it a house, she thought absently. "I'll sit outside my kids' rooms. I'd prefer you not go in there, and I already searched. They were clear."

They gave her a nod. She returned to her crouch in the hallway and reached for her phone, pushing the number for Gaines who answered with an endearing mumble.

"Jordy?"

"Hi, yes, sorry. Um, the police are here."

There was a shuffling sound, as if he abruptly sat up. "What? Baby, are you okay?"

"Yes, and the kids are fine. But I woke up to a man in my room."

"What?" he exclaimed, so loudly she had to tip the phone away from her ear. She could hear him shuffling some more, probably tossing clothes on.

"That's all I know for now. I woke up, he walked out, I checked the kids' rooms, and the police are here searching the *perimeter*."

"I'm going to be there in a few minutes. Do you want to stay on the phone with me?"

"I'll be fine. Please be careful, don't speed."

"Okay," he chuckled, clearly lying.

The police returned, looking grave. "I take it you didn't find him," Jordan whispered.

"No, and…"

Whatever he was going to say was interrupted by Gaines's arrival. The officers whirled, hands on guns, and Jordan sprang up.

"Sorry, that's my friend. I called him to come over. This is Gaines," she added as he eased closer and slid his arm around her waist, giving it a squeeze. It was hard not to melt into him a little. Jordan wasn't totally helpless, was pretty good at taking care of herself and the kids on a day-to-day basis. *But men, though.* There was something special about that little feeling of safety they gave, of letting go because you knew you were being taken care of. She'd had it with Jay, when he was home, and now she felt it again with Gaines because, unlike the officers, he had a personal interest in her wellbeing.

"Officers," Gaines said, nodding. "How's it going?"

"Well, we were telling the lady here that there were no signs of forced entry. Or exit. No discernable footprints, no disturbed vegetation. Is anything missing or amiss inside?"

"I haven't actually had a chance to look." Helplessly, she scanned the interior of the house. What would a burglar take? The most valuable thing she owned, besides the car, was an expensive stroller Jay's parents bought for Charlotte. "I can't imagine what that would be. We're not really into electronics."

"What about Jay's guns?" Gaines asked, giving her a squeeze.

"They're locked in the safe, as far as I know. Except the one…" she trailed helplessly away, swallowing hard.

"The one?" one of the officers prompted, suspicious now at the mention of a weapon.

Jordan cleared her throat. "The one he used to commit suicide a few weeks ago. That's still with you guys or the coroner's office or whoever handles those sorts of things." She tucked her hair behind her ears and let out a breath while the officers stared at her.

"I'm sorry for your loss," one of the officers said, but there was something new in his tone, a sort of *a-ha, so that's what this is,* kind of awareness. "We'll assign a car to drive by the rest of the night. Are you staying here?" Their attention turned to Gaines and Jordan felt like she was being handed off. *Here, capable man, take this crazy woman.*

"I'm staying," Gaines said with a nod.

"Call if you…have any more trouble," one of the officers said. The pause was small, but Jordan heard it. *Don't call for crazy reasons, only for something real.*

She nodded and thanked them. Now that Gaines was here and the adrenaline rush was over, she was anxious to have them out of her house, to move out of reach of their silent judgment.

She walked them to the door, closed it behind them and leaned on it, eyeing Gaines who eyed her in return.

CHAPTER 11

"Well, they think I'm crazy," Jordan declared.

Gaines laughed and shook his head. "Jordy, are you okay?"

"Okay for a crazy person, you mean?"

"No, I mean for a person who was awoken by someone in her room in the middle of the night and scared out of her wits." He eased toward her.

"You don't think I'm crazy?"

"I mean, you have questionable taste in movies and books and a disturbing amount of throw pillows on your bed. But do I think you're making up an intruder for attention? No way." He came to halt a foot away, which was an odd sort of distance. Too close to be casual, too far to be intimate. Jordan took a step away from the door, bringing her a tiny bit closer. His hand reached out and rested on her hip. They blinked at each other, both too surprised by the action to know what to do next. It was, without a doubt, the most intimate touch they'd ever exchanged.

He took a breath to speak and his phone beeped. "Hold on, that's Ridge." He dropped his hand as he pulled out his phone and swiped it.

"Are you with Jordan?" Ridge asked.

"Yes. How did you divine?"

"I had Blue set an alert on her house. I get a contact any time it comes up in an emergency."

"Can you CC me on that?" Ribs asked.

"Yep. Everything okay?"

"Yes. She had an intruder in her room. The locals couldn't find anything."

"Did you find anything?"

"I haven't looked yet, I'll let you know."

There was a pause, a significant one. "Maybe I better take a second look at Shimmer's suicide."

Ribs didn't say anything, but he agreed. If someone was targeting Jordan, there was a high likelihood that it was because of Shimmer's job. Otherwise why else?

They disconnected without saying goodbye and he shoved the phone back in his pocket.

"Does Cam think I'm crazy? Of course he does, dumb question," Jordan said, clasping her hands together in renewed misery.

Ribs smiled at her and clasped one of her hands, using it to lead her to the couch. "Let's sit and talk. You look all done in."

Self-consciously, she touched her hair. Who didn't look all done in in the middle of the night? Outside of Amelia and the supermodels he usually dated, that was.

They sat, side by side, thighs touching, her hand still firmly in his. His grasp was warm and reassuring and she shuddered, letting that reassurance wash over her and banish the last vestiges of fear. Noting the shudder, he switched her hand to his other one and used his newly free arm to slide around her shoulder, drawing her close.

"First of all no, Ridge does not think you're crazy. We've known you for over a decade. People don't suddenly start to make up phantom intruders."

She relaxed and rested her head on his chest. "That's nice." Which part was nice? His reassurance? His warm embrace? His rock-solid chest? Probably all of it. "There might be a little bit of precedent, though."

"How so?" he asked. His arm began to slide up and down her bicep and she lost the thread of the conversation for a few beats.

It's the middle of the night and a pretty man is touching you. Of course it's hard to think, she reassured herself. "A couple of weeks ago I thought I saw a man in my room." He tensed and she pressed her palm to his chest, urging him to hold off and relax until she continued. "It ended up being the vacuum. And I keep waking up, hearing sounds." She shook her head. "Maybe I really am losing it. I was so certain, though. I mean, I saw him, watched him walk out of my room. Didn't I?" She leaned back to assess his expression as he processed the flow of new information.

The new position put them within a hairsbreadth of each other, face to face. How was it even possible for him to look so good upon waking up? And why? Why was life so unfair, that men could roll out of bed and look like a Bowflex commercial and women had to do the full makeup and hair routine, not to mention the puffy under eye bags she'd been sporting since Charlotte was born.

"Jordy," he whispered. His finger reached out and began gently tracing her face.

"Mmm," she said and, oh no, did her eyes slide closed? Yes, yes they did. And apparently they were staying that way because she seemed unable to pry them open again, betraying how incredibly good the touch felt. Any touch felt good now, deprived as she was, but this was especially gentle and soothing.

"Walk me through it," Gaines said.

"Through what?"

"Tonight. What happened? What woke you?"

"Um," her thoughts seemed scattered all over the room now, put there by his gentle touch. She attempted to collect them and be coherent. "I woke up and saw the man and thought it was the vacuum again." *Good job being coherent, stupid.* "And then he walked out of the room."

"What did he look like?"

"Um," she said again, trying to remember. "It was dark, but I could tell it was a man because he was big."

"As big as me?" he asked.

"No one's as big as you," she said.

She couldn't see him, but somehow she knew he was smiling. "Short? Tall?"

"Tallish and kind of rounded somehow. Like not tall and broad shouldered like you and Jay. Tall and slumped. Maybe a tummy pooch."

"Hair?"

"I don't know if it had hair; he was wearing clothes."

He snorted. "Not the pooch, on his head. Blond? Dark?"

"Dunno. Too dark to see. All I had were impressions. Bigger, roundish, hunched, and then he walked out."

"How long between when he walked out and when you checked the kids' rooms?"

"Maybe a minute? I called the police and then ran into their rooms. The doors were open, though. I always close them."

His finger stilled, his body tensed. "You're sure they're okay?"

"Positive. I laid my hand on their chests and made sure I felt the steady rise and fall."

"Okay. I'm going to do my own perimeter sweep."

Her face creased into a smile.

"What?" he asked, preemptively smiling, too.

"You said 'perimeter.' Cop speak."

"Also spy speak," he reminded her. "Are you going to be okay here?"

"Fine," she assured him, eyes still closed.

"You're going to fall asleep, aren't you?" he guessed.

"I'm already there, dream fairy SEAL," she murmured.

With a chuckle, he withdrew his finger and went to check the house.

⚷

*H*e expected to find something. Not that he didn't have faith in the locals, because he did. But they were trained for different things. The police dealt with run of the mill morons who were stupid enough to rob someone in a snowstorm and leave tracks leading directly to their hideout. Ribs dealt with people who had fused off their fingerprints and wore cooling clothes to cloak their infrared signal. Even so, he found nothing.

His inspection of the perimeter was meticulous, but it didn't matter because there was nothing, not a whisper or hint that anyone had been there. He crouched beside Jordan's bedroom window, thinking.

As he saw it, there were three possibilities: Jordan, half-asleep and in a state of perpetual grief and stress, imagined an intruder. There was an intruder who made his entry and exit through the front door without leaving a trace and locking it behind him. Or there was an intruder, but he was so good at covering his tracks not even Ribs or the locals had caught a whiff. Absolutely none of those possibilities was a best-case scenario. As much as he didn't want to believe Jordan had a sophisticated intruder, he also didn't want to believe Jordan was delusional. Not for a minute did he believe she was making it up for attention, as the cops seemed inclined. He knew her too well, had known her too long to believe she would do anything like that. She was not now, nor had she ever been, the sort of person to seek attention. In fact being in the spotlight made her feel flustered, to the point where she became adorably awkward and clumsy.

Ribs realized he was still crouched and now grinning into the middle distance like a creepy psycho. He made himself stand and go back inside the house. Jordan was predictably asleep, slumped over on the couch in what had to be a miserable position. There was no use trying to wake her, however. Once she was out, she was out. Seemingly the only thing that could wake her was her kids, and both of them were silent. Ribs picked her up and carried her to her room. He laid her in the bed and tucked the covers over her. She curled into a little ball and, unable to resist, he reached out and smoothed his hand over her hair, smiling when she gave an annoyed little huff and shimmied into a tighter ball.

He eased out of the room and checked on both kids, pausing at the entry to their rooms to let his eyes scan. Everything seemed as it should be, but he still felt uneasy, like something was off. Then again everything had felt off since Shimmer's death, so perhaps it was merely that same pervading sense of wrongness and not something more.

Reassured that at least the kids were well and truly asleep, he went to the living room and stared at the couch, frowning. It felt far, too far, from Jordan. Though his mind told him she was fine, he didn't feel like being separated. So he tugged the afghan from the back of the sofa, went back to Jordan's bedroom, lay down on the floor, and fell immediately asleep.

Jordan woke with a start, as she had been doing since Jay's passing. Adrenaline slammed through her and she couldn't remember why, and then it came flooding back. She had woken already this night, to an intruder in her room. But before the fear and terror could take root, a new sort of peace washed over her because somehow she knew Gaines was still in the house. And if Gaines was in the house, she was safe.

It was so sudden and complete, that feeling of safety, that Jordan almost wept, not only with the shock of it but with the absolute relief of not being the one in charge, of not having to take care of anything for a little while. She might have fallen back into an exhausted sleep, except that now her bladder was awake and demanding attention.

Could she put it off?

No, she could not. The harder she tried to ignore it, the more urgent it became. There was no help for it; she would have to slog to the potty and would probably stay awake the rest of the night. *I'll sleep again when the children are grown*, she assured herself. It had become her survival mantra. *I'll go for dental and vision checkups when the children are grown. I'll figure out what makeup color I should be wearing when the kids are grown. I'll go shopping and find clothes that fit well when the kids are grown. I'll take a shower or bath by myself when the kids are grown.*

I'll be able to sit down and eat an entire meal when the kids are grown. My car will not look like a hoarder's paradise when the kids are grown. She would do all the things other functioning adults did, someday when the kids were grown.

For instance, she would learn how to walk across the floor and not trip, as she did now, going down, down, down as the floor rushed gladly up to greet her.

CHAPTER 12

Even in the midst of plummeting she smothered her yelp, not wanting to wake the children and alarm them. Instead Jordan braced herself for an impact that never came.

Strong arms tucked around her, taking the impact of her fall as they rolled, landing side by side and pressed firmly together.

"Hey, what's up?" Gaines asked. His voice was husky with sleep because of course it was. Only a guy like him could be awakened by a clumsy female tripping over him and somehow turn it into a smolder.

"Nothing much," Jordan said, still breathless from her near miss disaster.

Gaines laughed and laid his head down. On her shoulder.

Should I pet him? I want to pet him, she thought before quickly banishing the thought. If she began petting her husband's friend's head in the middle of the night, it would certainly be the final stop on the full psychosis train with absolutely no redemption. Instead she sniffed, inhaling his manly scent so it went to the very bottom of her lungs and sent tingles of estrogen all through her. *Sniff him, that's less creepy. Good thinking. Why don't you reach over and snip a segment of his hair, really stick the landing.*

It was just that he smelled so good and he was so warm and strong and Jordan was so tired and everything seemed like pure chaos all the time. It wasn't that she was actually attracted to Gaines, not in that way. Was she?

"I'm sorry I kicked your spleen," she whispered.

He laughed again and stifled it by pressing his lips. To her shoulder. As one does. When cuddled together on the floor. Of her bedroom. "Jordy, you're a loon."

Yes, there, that. Back to normal. Because absolutely no one could be having sexy thoughts compatible with being a loon.

"Gaines," she began in a whisper. "I think I know what's going on here."

His eyes popped open and he stared at her, frozen. "You do?"

She nodded. "You feel sorry for me...since Jay. And I think it's so sweet, you reaching out like this. But I'm doing okay, I really am." Unable to resist, she reached out and smoothed her hand over his head. *To soften the blow and make him understand I'm grateful,* she assured herself. *Not because his hair is thicker and more touchable than should be humanly possible. How has he not been in a conditioner commercial by now?*

Gaines smiled until his eyes crinkled and then tugged her closer, snugging her tight against his chest as his face burrowed against her neck. "Oh, Jordy," he murmured.

And now Jordan was a tad confused. His tone was exasperated, but his body was...not? "I'm a little confused," she said slowly because, again, not complaining. His solid good-smelling warmth was the best thing that had happened to her in forever. "Are you snuggling me?"

He sat up slightly and stared down at her, looking uncharacteristically pensive. "Yes," he said, but it came out like a question, with a slight upturn at the end.

Jordan nodded. "Right, right, sure, okay. It's just...why, though?"

He bit his lip. He was a two hundred pound former SEAL turned spy and he was lying on her floor in he middle of the night biting his lip in uncertainty and Jordan didn't think she had ever seen anything more adorable. It was like when a Great Dane accidentally brushed by a leaf and jumped away in panic.

Gaines cleared his throat. "The truth is, Jordan, that I, uh...I..." He stared at her, hopelessly lost, helplessly unable to continue.

He needs a rescue, Jordan thought, which was surprising but also sort of a relief. It wasn't often in her life now that she got to be able to be the one lending a hand up. "Are you maybe having a hard time and cuddling helps?"

He nodded, latching on to her statement with palpable relief. "Yes, but also..." He took a breath and let it out in a huff, like Jay used to do when he was getting ready to lift a particularly heavy weight. "But also..." he tried, and then looked at her imploringly again.

"Also..." What? What did she know about Gaines? She put the pieces together, all the times he had picked up her kids and covered them with kisses, all the times he had hugged Jay and her goodbye and hello after a separation. And the light bulb went off. "Also you're naturally affectionate and you *like* to snuggle." How had she never understood that fact before? Gaines was a teddy bear, but of course he hadn't snuggled her before because she had been married. But now he was using it as a form of affection to soothe them both. It made perfect sense.

"Yes," he said, a puff of air that once again sounded like total relief. He nodded, his hands unconsciously gripping her tighter.

Jordan stared at him, reorienting her brain around the new normal. "So we're...cuddle buddies now?" she tried, eking the words out slowly like a rope, in case she needed to yank them back.

Gaines nodded, relaxing a little. "I guess, if that's okay? Is that okay? Is it too weird to be like this with me?"

He had to be joking. Had he seen him? He was possibly the most beautiful man she had ever seen in real life, chiseled jaw, ridiculous hair, full lips, ripped body. She had known him for thirteen years, seen almost every iteration of his personality, knew he was solid and dependable and good, down to his core. And he was asking if she *minded horribly* if they snuggled. She couldn't help it, she snorted a giggle. And then, once the door was open, had no hope of stopping the others.

"What's your brain doing?" Gaines asked because, truth be told, he knew her pretty well, too.

She shook her head, face pressed against his solid chest to try and push back the laughter. "I'll try to manage, Gaines," she choked, gasping for breath between near-hysterical laughter. "I'll try hard to overcome my revulsion and touch you." To prove her point, she slid her arms around his neck and shifted her face to his neck, fitting it in that perfect little spot men kept on reserve for women.

"Same, Jordy, same," Gaines whispered, now smoothing his hand down the back of her hair.

It was so soothing, so gentle, so filled to the brim with tender affection that Jordan fell almost immediately asleep, her full bladder miraculously forgotten.

⚷

Gaines woke first, which was a special sort of agony because it meant he had time to enjoy the moment of waking with Jordan beside him. *Jordan beside him.* His mind couldn't quite comprehend that the thing he had denied himself from wanting so long had finally happened.

All those years ago, when Jordan and Shimmer were dating, he hadn't been quite so magnanimous. There were times, many times, when he envied his friend. When he'd felt bitter jealousy, when he'd had dreams of pushing Shimmer over a short cliff. In an abstract sort of way, of course. He never really would have offed Jay. But that resentment had been hard to tame. And then they got married and it wasn't fun and games anymore. Gaines was not the sort of man who wanted another man's wife, and especially not his best friend. So he had worked hard to shove everything aside, to compartmentalize his feelings for Jordan, to rearrange and tame them into a workable friendship. And he had succeeded. Never once in the last twelve years had he felt that same sort of envy or resentment. Shimmer and Jordan were settled, a done deal. She was off limits forever.

Except now she wasn't, and where was he to go with that? He felt like everything he had stuffed into that box so long ago had now sprung free and grown legs. But he had no idea what to do with it. He had spent so many years taming his feelings and thoughts and desires where she was concerned, always reminding himself what was inappropriate, that he now had no frame of reference for what was appropriate.

The kids were an easy matter. They would always be Jay's, and Gaines would always love them as such. He had no thoughts about usurping Jay's role in their life, only guarding and protecting it. He wanted the kids to know their dad, to understand the brave and upstanding person he'd been. He wanted to guide and nurture them like a true uncle, shepherding them safely into adulthood.

But Jordan.

Was it wrong to want her now again? Or rather still? Because his feelings for her had never gone away. They had been tamed into something manageable and appropriate, but they had never disappeared. But Jay was barely gone. Wasn't it wrong to swoop in this way? Was he swooping if he was being invited? Maybe that was the problem. What were Jordan's feelings on the matter? Of course she saw him as a friend; they had known each other and been pals for thirteen years. Right now she was mired in grief, but was there hope for someday? Or would Gaines once again have to try and box up his feelings for her and pack them away?

A shuffling sound alerted him. His head whipped toward the door and he smiled. Nash had apparently learned to get out of his crib and was now crawling toward them, about to enter on the threshold of the room. Would he be distressed by Gaines's presence in his mother's room? But no, he didn't notice Gaines at all, so intent was he on reaching his target. Gaines didn't realize what that was until he reached Jordan, lifted her shirt, and latched on.

Gaines thought his eyes were probably like saucers. He'd been in the room with Jordan when she nursed, but she had been discreet. If he hadn't known she was nursing, he wouldn't know she was nursing. Nash, however, had no concerns with discretion as he lifted his mother's shirt and chowed down. Gaines got an eyeful and shifted his focus to the ceiling, blushing. Or maybe flushing. There was an image he did not need to see and would now be unable to get out of his head.

At least it answered one question for him: if Jordan rebuffed him, he would be unable to return to the friendzone. They were at an all-or-nothing point here, and that scared him as much as it made him sad. He could not, would not abandon her in her time of need. But if he told her he loved her, as he had tried to do last night, and she didn't feel the same, he also couldn't stay. *It's better to remain where I am, stuck in the in between.* For both their sakes he would continue to linger in the gray zone. He would be a friend. He would take care of her. And he would keep his deeper feelings to himself, cuddle buddies or not.

Nash finished his breakfast and crawled away to play with the laundry basket, leaving Jordan completely exposed. Gaines didn't mind. He really, *really* didn't mind, but she would die if she woke up and realized what happened. Gently and without looking, he reached over and righted her shirt, pulling it down so she was completely covered. Then he used that same arm to dab his sweaty forehead. If he could survive being this close to Jordan and pretending to feel nothing more than friendship, he could survive anything. And definitely deserved some sort of medal, he added as Jordan curled toward him, nestling her soft curves against the entire length of his body.

CHAPTER 13

When Jordan woke, she made breakfast. She felt more than a little confused and having something concrete to do made her feel better.

She had slept. On the floor. With *Gaines*. Nothing happened, but still. Was it weird? Or was it weird because it didn't feel weird? It had felt natural. More than natural, it had felt *nice*. Jordan didn't know if that feeling was particular to Gaines or merely the relief at having a man in the house again. With him there, she hadn't suffered even a moment of fear. She hadn't realized how fitful her rest had been until she had solid sleep again. After she lay down with Gaines, she had basically fallen into a coma, only waking when Charlotte shook her shoulder. *Did Nash nurse on me when I was asleep?* The uneven feeling in her body told her yes. When she nursed, she switched sides so she wouldn't feel lopsided. After she woke she felt so lopsided she had to pump the fuller-feeling side, but how had she slept through that? More distressing, had Gaines?

He woke before she did and, to her surprise, remained lying next to her. *Probably didn't want to wake you. He's polite that way.* When Charlotte shook her on the shoulder, he offered her a chagrined smile.

"I tried to distract her, but she wouldn't be dissuaded. These kids love and need their mama," he had whispered.

"I…also…am," she had whispered back, addled by the sight of him so near her face first thing in the morning. Not only did she not wake up coherent, she knew for a fact there was no way she looked as good as he did. Maybe no one did. Maybe he'd been genetically modified to wake up beautiful, a GMO SEAL, some sort of government experiment to save the world and make women feel bad about their under eye bags and belly pudge in one fell swoop.

Gaines doesn't care how you look because he doesn't see you that way, she told herself. She told herself again as she cooked breakfast, Gaines's gaze steadfast on her as she moved. He seemed intent. She wondered why until he spoke and dispelled the mystery.

"Thanks for doing this, Jordy. No one cooks for me."

Ah, food. Jay loved food, and so did all of his friends. It was their love language, especially anything grilled. Much like with dogs, if you give a SEAL a steak, he's your friend for life.

"I'll cook for you anytime," she promised, smile slipping when Gaines regarded her with what she had come to recognize as his smolder.

"I'd like that," he replied. His tone was even, but his eyes…

Jordan turned away, flustered, and promptly singed her hand on the edge of the pan. She hissed and shook out her fingers, intending to move on, but Gaines was beside her, already inspecting her hand.

"What happened?"

"Burned it a little," she said, staring at him instead of her hand. He was concerned about her hand, her tiny little hand, and it was such an anomaly she couldn't wrap her head around it. No one had taken notice of her small wounds since she was a child. Jay hadn't been the doting type, and after the kids came along, Jordan naturally shoved down everything in favor of them. Stubbed toes, broken nails, and even burned hands fell so low on the priority list she barely noted them anymore.

But now Gaines was inspecting her hand like it might turn septic as he led her to the faucet and ran it under cold water. And the shock of it, both the water and the fact that someone was taking care of her, felt so good tears sprang to her eyes.

After the soothing water ran over it for a while, he dried her hand, patting it gently with the towel, then broke off a piece of her half-dead aloe plant and rubbed it over the wound like a salve. All the while Jordan stared at him, fascinated and gobsmacked. She had spent so much of the last decade keeping everything together, centering herself around Jay and his job and now the children. She had no idea until this moment how many pieces of herself she had lost.

Gaines finished his tender ministrations to her hand, looked up, and blinked. They stared at each other, frozen. Jordan swallowed hard.

"You're good in an emergency," she whispered.

"Sort of what they pay me for," he whispered in return.

"Thank you," she added.

He wrapped her hand in both his, swaddling it. "Keep it safe today."

Jordan's brain seemed unable to fathom a reply. When Jay died, she automatically added it to the things she would have to power through and endure. There was no time to mourn with two small children underfoot, one of whom still depended on her for literal nourishment. Jay's parents and her mother flitted in and back out after a few days, returning to their homes far away. It never once occurred to her someone else might come along and help shoulder the burden, might pay attention to *her*, might try to take care of *her*. It was so unexpected and out of her comfort zone that her mind couldn't seem to process it. So she simply stared at Gaines, seeing him anew, not as Jay's best friend, but as her friend, someone she could talk to and count on.

She wondered if Gaines guessed a little of her thoughts because he brushed a finger on her cheek and gave her a reassuring smile. Jordan turned her head to the side so he wouldn't see the tears that smile wrought, but too late because he dropped her hand and pulled her into an enveloping hug. His arms swallowed her, cocooning her against him. Her ear pressed to his heart and her arms slid around his solid waist and she released some tears, only a few, not enough to relieve the deep ache inside her. But enough to release a bit of the pressure that had been building since Jay's funeral.

Gaines kissed the top of her head and rested his raspy cheek on it, and everything about the moment was so soothing. It was almost like taking a warm bath. Maybe better because she didn't have to worry and wonder if the kids were okay. They sat calmly eating cheerios while Jordan received what was arguably the best hug of her life, if only for its restorative properties. But the fact that Gaines was solid and warm and smelled good didn't hurt her feelings.

"You're going to be okay," Gaines whispered, rubbing a gentle little circle in the middle of her back.

Was she? She had no idea, but she trusted Gaines's opinions on things. If she was truly in danger of falling apart, he wouldn't placate her. Maybe he could see a future for her where she ceased to be on autopilot, where she could think and feel and function again.

"You're nice," she declared, tipping her head back to peer up at him.

"To you, for certain," he said. He touched his nose to hers and they froze again, sharing another one of those what-is-happening-here gazes. This time they were interrupted by Nash who tossed his sippy cup of water on the floor, spilling it everywhere.

"My doggie will get it," Charlotte declared and then, before either of them could stop her, shoved her stuffed dog's face into the sopping mess. Then, realizing her dog was now soaked, burst into noisy tears and propelled herself at Jordan.

"And we're back," Jordan murmured. Gaines helpfully cleaned the spilled water and volunteered to keep an eye on Nash while Jordan tossed Charlotte's dog into the dryer. After that she resumed making breakfast. They ate in peace, the sort of peace that comes from the comfort of being long acquaintances who already had a lot of shared meals under their belts. It was comforting and restorative, but at the same time poignant because Jay should have been there, eating and laughing with them. They both felt the lack, and yet the fact that they shared their melancholy brought even more comfort.

"I should get to work," Gaines declared. He sounded as reluctant to go as Jordan felt to have him leave. With him there, she felt the security that had been lacking since Jay died. Now, as he put on his shoes, the gnawing ache of loneliness threatened to return with a vengeance, making it hard to breathe. Gaines paused, eyeing her in concern. "I could take the day off."

She laughed and shook her head. "No, you couldn't. You'd be thinking about it all day, feeling bad, wondering what was going down while you were here."

She had him there. His life was basically his job, and it had become hard to separate the two. "I'll be fine," Jordan added, hoping she sounded more confident than she felt. *I'm just tired,* she assured herself. It had been a sleepless night after a restless few weeks. Of course it was natural to yearn when you were depleted. The more worrisome thing was that she couldn't seem to put a name to what she yearned for. Comfort? Care? Security? Affection? She hadn't had those things since Jay died, and some not for a while before.

Gaines reached out and clasped her hand, giving it a squeeze. His hand was warm and reassuring. She didn't want to let go, when it was time to pull away, and that was concerning. *Pull it together, Jordan. Gaines is not your security blanket.* She made herself release him by focusing on securing her messy bun.

"Call me. If you hear anything, see anything, or for any reason."

She nodded. She didn't want to say she'd be fine again because it would sound untrue. And she did think she'd be fine, as long as she didn't spend too long thinking about last night—about the man she saw or maybe hadn't, about tripping over Gaines and then waking up next to him.

Belatedly she realized she was once again staring at Gaines who stared at her in return in what was becoming a common series of loaded moments. And then Nash intervened once again, tossing both his sippie cup of water and his handful of smashed cheerios onto the floor.

Gaines regarded the mess, gearing up to intervene, when Jordan put up a halting hand. "Go. Save yourself. Once you get sucked in, you'll never leave."

He stood and kissed her cheek. *That's what I'm counting on,* he thought but was smart enough not to say.

CHAPTER 14

"Well, well, well." Eliza sat at her desk sipping something blue with bubbles. That was how Ribs knew he was getting old, because he had no idea what she was drinking, nor did he want to.

"Why is your drink blue?" he mused, pausing to frown at it.

"Blue pea," she said.

"Probably, after you drink that," Logan added. Ribs snorted a laugh as Eliza tossed a paperclip at Logan's head.

"It's delicious and nutritious and most of all beautiful, but I wouldn't expect you goons to appreciate drink art," Eliza sniffed.

"You'd be right," Logan muttered, dodging another paperclip. Ribs attempted to slip through their bickering unnoticed, but no such luck.

"Not done with you," Eliza called, and he paused as she waved her hand expansively in his direction. "I couldn't help but note that you're wearing the same clothes as yesterday."

"So am I," Logan added helpfully.

"That's because you're a degenerate who lacks your own washer and dryer. Gaines, though. Gotta be a girl involved." She sat back, letting the straw of her blue drink rest lazily on the side of her mouth.

"Nah. A friend called in the night with a problem, and I had to go over." He swiped his hand up and down on his face a few times, his palm making a rasping sound on his beard stubble. Apparently he looked as rough as he felt. *When did I get so decrepit that a night of lost sleep made me feel this bad?* Back in the day he could stay awake for days, and had. Now he missed out on a few hours and felt like he'd been run through a gristmill head first. If he felt this bad, he couldn't imagine how much worse off Jordan must be, she who had been missing sleep the last three years.

"A girlfriend," Eliza said, using a ruler to reach out and poke his bicep.

"A girl who is a friend," Ribs amended.

"No, you don't have those," Eliza declared, making a slurping noise as she reached the end of her drink.

"What? Of course I do," he argued.

"Nope," she said. She opened the drink and began tilting the bubbles toward her face.

"Uh, hello," he said, pointing between them.

She paused and regarded him with what seemed to be a cynical stare. "Where do I live?"

He froze.

"What are my hobbies?

He blinked.

"Do I have a boyfriend?"

His feet shifted.

She set aside her drink with a sigh and rested her hands on her desk. "We are coworkers. Friendly coworkers, yes, but not exactly friends. You don't have female friends."

"But I do," he insisted.

"The wives of all your buddies?" she guessed.

He paused, hating to admit it. "Yes."

"Anyone who's not a wife of a friend?"

He paused again. "No. But what's wrong with that?"

"Nothing, it's how it is. You're not friend guy. Logan, on the other hand." She motioned toward Logan. "So deep in the Friendzone he bought land and is thinking of building."

"True story," Logan said, so unconcerned he didn't bother to look up at them.

"I don't understand," Ribs said, looking uncertainly between Logan and Eliza.

"You're just that guy," Eliza said, flicking her fingers at him. "You're all buff and pretty, used to be a SEAL, now you're a spy. I bet in high school you were soooo athletic." She rolled her eyes.

"Yes. What's wrong with any of that?"

"Nothing. But you'll never be friend guy. Don't invade our turf." She motioned between Logan and herself.

Ribs scratched his temple, more than a little confused. "I don't understand this whole conversation."

Eliza leaned forward, resting more of her weight on her forearms. A professor about to begin deep instruction. "It's like this, Gaines. You're the hero, we're the sidekick support team. And that's okay. But the hero isn't that guy who has *friends*," here she paused and rolled her eyes. "He's the one who saves the damsel in distress. Be realistic. This woman, whoever she is, is about to be a conquest. She's the damsel in distress and you're the hero. Own it. I bet she's blond and beautiful, even at three in the morning. She is, isn't she? I'm right. Tell me I'm right." She bit her lip, anxiously awaiting his response.

Ribs thought of Jordan, hair splayed around her face, cheeks still a soft shade of pink, even as she slept. She still looked like that wholesome farm girl, all these years later. Somehow, since having kids, she'd grown even more beautiful and he finally understood why: it was the expression on her face, the absolute rapture of love when she looked at them, the pure and unadulterated delight she took in them.

"She...she...she..." he stuttered, staring into space, heart thumping like crazy with the sudden and intense desire to walk out of the building, drive back to Jordan, gather her up, breathe her in, make her understand everything that could be between them.

When he blinked and came back to earth, Eliza and Logan were both staring at him, mouths ajar.

"Uh-oh," Eliza breathed.

"What?" he said, a weary sigh. Eliza was a lot of work. Most days he didn't mind, but today he didn't have the energy for it.

"You flipped the script," she said softly, wonderingly.

"What?" he said, opening his eyes to squint at her.

"The girl, she's not your usual variety," she said.

He shifted again. "How could you possibly know that?"

"I know everything," she said, which was annoyingly true. Not only was she a computer genius, but she seemed to possess some sort of sixth sense that often alerted her to things before they happened. When they were working a job and Eliza warned him things were about to go south, he listened. So far she had a hundred percent accuracy with her dire predictions.

"What do you know?" he croaked, because that was how desperate he was. Even Eliza's cutting sarcasm began to sound appealing, if it offered him hope.

"She's smart and sweet and..." she paused, squinting at his face. *"Normal."*

"Everyone I date is normal," he argued, rasping his hand on his stubble again.

Eliza quirked an eyebrow toward Logan. "Logan, tell me about the women Gaines goes out with."

"Pretty much every one of them could be in my fantasy folder marked, 'Would Not Put Me Out If I Were On Fire.'"

Now Eliza's attention swung back to Ribs. "This girl, would she stop and shoot the breeze with Logan?"

Gaines pictured Jordan in the office, pausing to talk to everyone. She would love Eliza and Logan because she loved strange people, the quirkier the better. "She'd probably invite you over for supper," he rasped. Why did this entire conversation make him so uncomfortable? Maybe because it tread dangerously close to things he'd never talked about or acknowledged before. Jordan was different from other women in his life, in a separate folder, to borrow Logan's vernacular. Except Gaines's folders would be marked, "Ideal Woman" and "Everyone Else." Needless to say Jordan was the only woman in the first folder, the only woman who had ever inhabited it.

Now it was Eliza's turn to groan and press her hand to her eyes.

"What?" Ribs asked, alarmed.

"It turns out you're not as shallow as I thought and now maybe I'm attracted to you, too," she said.

He rolled his eyes at her absurdity, certain she was lying for dramatic effect. "I think Harry Potter's name and all supporting character's should be wiped from the earth," he said.

She dropped her hand and scowled at him. "And we're back. Also, how dare you." She leaned forward to adjust the little Harry Potter figurine attached to her computer, whispering, "He didn't mean it, Potter."

"Are we done torturing me today? Because I have stuff to do," he said. He gestured helplessly toward his office but before he could take a step away, Eliza hailed him back.

"Wait, Gaines, for real. I have to tell you something."

He paused and turned serious eyes on her because she had the tone, the I-don't-know-how-I-know-but-something-bad-is-about-to-happen tone. He balled his fists and braced, for what he had no idea. "What?"

Her face worked itself into a frown, head tipped as she studied him. "This girl..."

"She's a woman, a year younger than me," Ribs interjected.

She gave an approving little nod as if it somehow agreed with what she was about to say. "This woman, she has no idea how you feel."

"Good because we're just friends," he said.

She quirked an eyebrow at him.

He huffed a sigh and shrugged. "Fine, I maybe like her a little." *Liar, big fat liar.* "But for a lot of reasons it's better if we remain only friends right now."

"But someday..." Eliza prompted.

He sighed again, longsuffering. There was no law stating he had to keep this conversation going, but he couldn't seem to stop it because Eliza seemed like she was about to bestow secret wisdom on him, information that might one day come in handy. He couldn't resist. "Someday, maybe..." Someday maybe every secret dream he'd had for the last thirteen years would finally come true. His heart was lub dubbing painfully again, not the same sort of fast staccato it performed when he was in the middle of an adrenaline rush. More like that painful thump it gave when he looked at his parents and realized how much they'd aged between visits. Or when Charlotte presented him with some new milestone she'd achieved in his absence. It was a mix of love and wanting and pain and joy he couldn't begin to understand, a feeling that went too deep for articulation.

"You have to be clear with her, more clear than you've ever been. You have to make her understand. It won't be enough that you know and think she should also know. You have to spell it out for her, word for word, probably more than once. Hints won't be enough."

"Why not?" he asked, and now his heart began to move into the adrenaline phase because, holy geez, actually telling Jordan. Could he ever do that?

"Because guys like you..."

"Trying really hard not to be offended by that intro," he interjected.

"Because guys like you tend to have a type, and 'nice girl' isn't it. All I'm saying is, if you want things to work, be clear in your intentions," Eliza said and then, with a dismissive little nod, returned her attention to her work.

Ribs remained staring at her a few beats, processing. His eyes swiveled to Logan. "Anything to add?"

"If she turns you down, can I have her? Because I also have a type, and heartbroken nice girl is at the tippy top of my list."

"I will literally break all the bones in your hands and make it look like an accident if you ever even think of making anything more than eye contact with her," Ribs said, tone perfectly even. Logan was the kind of guy Jordan would go for, though. A guy whose face matched his personality—painfully nice, like Shimmer.

"Noted. BRB, going to change into some clean underwear," Logan said and slipped away from his desk.

"Well, I think things are about to get very interesting," Eliza said, beaming her approval on him. "Come back if you need more help or advice from the love doctor."

Ribs opened his mouth to protest, realized he couldn't because he felt rather desperate for help, and turned and walked to his office, closing the door with a sigh of relief.

"Jordan, woo-hoo, Jordan."

Jordan's neighbor waved at her from across their adjoining lawns. Jordan waved back halfheartedly and with a sinking feeling. It wasn't that she didn't like her neighbors, a retired couple where the wife's overt friendliness ran counter to her husband's recalcitrance. Rather it was that it had taken a half hour to wrangle the kids into their clothes and stroller. Jordan had enough snacks to keep them entertained for a thirty-minute jog, if she was lucky. Talking to her chatty neighbor would use up much of that precious snack time. Her jiggly mom pooch burbled, reminding her of its resentment over the pending workout and determination to linger and grow.

"Hello, Nan, Kurt," Jordan said, nodding. Nan, she learned during their first conversation, retired last year from her job as a middle school secretary. She had no idea what Kurt retired from, but it appeared to be something in the government or military, if the cagey way he studied her and his environment was any indication. He remained at attention beside his wife, scanning the quiet street around them like it might erupt into chaos without his scrutiny. Living so close to DC meant most of the people she encountered seemed to have some connection to the government in one way or another.

"Hi, sweetie. How are you?" Nan tipped her head in a way that was becoming familiar to Jordan. She thought maybe it was pity, but she tried to take it as concern instead.

"I'm doing well," Jordan said. "These two keep me busy." She glanced down at Nash, already halfway through his pile of jogging snacks.

"We were a bit worried after the police showed up last night," Nan said, tone leading.

Here is a woman who knows how to gossip, Jordan thought. Nan had perfected the balance between nosiness and care. In other words, she knew how to ask intrusive questions cloaked in sincerity. "I thought I heard something, an intruder," Jordan admitted, cheeks flushing. She didn't want these people to know the embarrassing truth—that she wasn't certain there had been an intruder. When Kurt's eyes flicked toward her and narrowed, the flush deepened.

"Oh, no," Nan said, pressing her hand to her cheek with a gasp. "Is everything okay?"

Jordan shrugged one shoulder. "The police came. They made a thorough search and didn't see anything." Jordan trailed helplessly away, gaze slipping to her house. Was she crazy? Was her imagination that overheated? The police certainly thought so.

Kurt made a little harrumph sound, drawing her attention back to him. When she looked at him, his lips were pressed tightly together in disapproval, eyes still on the horizon. What did that mean? Did he also think she was crazy? That she was a hysterical female who had wasted valuable police time?

"I saw another car, a strange car here overnight." Nan was at it again, comingling a mass dose of nosiness with half-hearted worry, an eighty/twenty ratio at this point.

"I called one of my husband's friends to come over. He stayed after the police left, to make certain everything was okay," she added weakly when Nan's brows rose and Kurt's lips all but disappeared.

How much farther could they retract in disapproval before he swallowed them?

"Oh," Nan said, drawing out the word to eight syllables, each one dripping with judgment.

"If you'll excuse me, the kids and I were going to go for a little jog." She glanced at Nash's stroller tray, now populated by a mere three rice puffs.

"Sure," Nan said. She still stared at Jordan who could practically hear the story repeat itself to her friends. *My neighbor gal, a recent widow, called her husband's friend to come stay the night. A* MONTH *after he died. Tsk, tsk, tsk.*

What was more disconcerting was her husband's expression, now also narrowed speculatively on Jordan. She didn't think he judged her for having Gaines stay, didn't believe he cared one way or another what she did with her personal life. His look seemed to be trying to convey something, but what? And why did it leave her fighting a shudder as she turned and jogged away?

Twenty minutes later, dripping with sweat and fielding two noisy children, who had finished their snacks and wanted out, she forgot her neighbors, forgot everything but trying to keep the kids quiet and entertained in the stroller as she trudged back home. Why did the stroller always feel light on the way somewhere and leaden on the way back?

When she opened the door and stepped inside, it took her another five minutes of unbuckling and unloading the stroller to stand up straight and come to a complete halt.

The door wasn't locked when she let herself in.

She had locked the door when she let herself out. Hadn't she?

Her mind whirred, struggling to remember. She'd worked up a sweat trying to get the oversized stroller over the threshold, had paused, turned toward the house and... Her mind went blank with sudden panic because she couldn't remember. Today's exit overlaid itself with every other exit. She always locked the door and double checked it. Had she done that today or was she remembering some other time? If she didn't lock it, how could she be so careless, today of all days? And if she did lock it, how did it get unlocked again?

"Hello," she called into the echoing stillness. Her senses felt hyper alert. Did it smell funny, or was that her overheated brain?

"Mommy, who are you talking to?" Charlotte asked, tipping her head curiously toward Jordan like a baby bird.

"No one, sweetie. Charlotte, do you remember if Mommy locked the door on the way out?"

Charlotte shrugged one bitty shoulder, attention already diverted to the stuffed dog that hadn't accompanied them on the jog.

Jordan pulled out her phone and stared at it, debating texting Gaines. What could she possibly tell him? *I may or may not have locked the door? I'm disturbed because my house is calm and settled but something smells a little funky?*

Probably your bad housekeeping skills again, she chided herself. The trash needed to go out, the spoiled food needed removed from the fridge. Tomorrow was trash day and there were dirty diapers in the wastebasket of Nash's room. Of *course* it smelled bad. It would be shocking if it didn't.

In the end Jordan texted Gaines but left out all the crazy.

Thanks for showing up and staying last night. I hope you're having a good day after weathering a night on my hard floor.

He replied immediately, which was somehow so surprising she dropped her phone in a flustered startle. *Anytime, Jordy, you know that. And it turns out it doesn't matter if the floor is hard if the company is soft.*

Jordan's jaw dropped. Was Gaines…flirting with her? Blushing at the ridiculous thought, she shook her head and blew out a breath, laughing at herself. Of course Gaines was not flirting with her. He was simply one of those men, one who was so charming everything he said ended up sounding flattering and appealing.

Trying to infuse her text tone with lightness, she returned, *If that was your idea of a good time, we need to get you out more, sailor.*

The effect was ruined when Gaines instantly replied, *It's a date,* with a winking emoji.

"My goodness," Jordan whispered, stuffing her phone in her pocket so she wouldn't be tempted to reply and bumble into awkwardness. He was undoubtedly kidding. They were pals and things were comfortable between them. That was all this was, for certain. Because she knew, down to her marrow, that she and Gaines were all wrong for each other. He was too perfect, too beautiful. And she was…

She glanced down at her yoga pants, noting a stain on her faded t-shirt. She was sort of a disaster, more so now that she was a widow. *Perfect is not for me,* she reminded herself. At this point in her exhausted life cycle, she would happily settle for uneventful.

The kids began to clamor loudly for lunch and, forgetting everything but motherhood and the long day ahead, she folded the stroller and went to the kitchen, not thinking again about the mystery of her unlocked door.

⚷

*D*espite Ribs's assurances to Jordan, he felt the pain of the sleepless night all day. So much that he pulled out his phone and texted Ethan.

When's the last time you slept on the floor?

When Amelia and I bought the new place, before our stuff arrived.

How'd it go? Ribs asked. Was it just him? Were his fellow SEAL guys still as fit as they used to be?

Couldn't lift my left leg all the way for a week, Ethan replied, putting Gaines's mind to rest.

How much longer can we stay in the game? Ribs asked him.

I'm getting out, as soon as we have kids. I want to be present, coach soccer, all the things.

What will you do? Ribs asked.

Amelia's thinking of going solo, opening her own salon, maybe taking on a few employees. She already makes more than I do. I'll stay home and she'll support for a while, until the kids are older and I figure out a next step.

Ribs read the text three times and remained staring at his phone. Ethan, daring, never met an adventure he didn't take *Ethan,* was actively planning a future that included himself as a stay-at-home dad? Ribs honestly didn't know how he felt about that. They'd spent years, no, *decades* training to do what they did. How did someone walk away so easily? Or was it easy?

Really? he finally replied.

When you have kids, someone has to raise them. Might as well be me.

You really think you can walk away? Ribs tried.

For anything else? No. For Amelia and our family? I'd leave today.

Ribs remained staring at his phone again. How did a man get to that point? What did it take? Because he knew for certain he wasn't there. Would he ever be?

His thumb skittered over his phone and a picture popped up. It was Jordan in the hospital, just after she had Nash. She lay holding him in one arm, her other curled around Charlotte, beaming as she looked at her kids. Seeing her that way, so beautiful, perfect, and happy, was like a gut punch. Had he seen her smile that way since that day? For the last few months she'd looked so strained, stressed, and exhausted. Suddenly it didn't seem to be enough to see her smile again if he wasn't the one who put it there. But how could he do that when his life was a revolving door of assignments?

Charlotte's party loomed in the future and Ribs set it as an honorary deadline for himself. By then he wanted to have an answer or a plan, maybe both. It was an ambitious goal, figuring how clueless he now felt. But he hadn't gotten where he was by being laid back and waiting for life to come to him. An answer wouldn't present itself; he would have to go out and find it. And he would. Just as soon as he figured out where to start looking.

CHAPTER 16

Baking with children was always better in theory. In Jordan's imagination, she and Charlotte would bond enviously, like something from a Hallmark commercial, as they mixed up a batch of cookies. In reality Charlotte dumped four eggs on the floor when she hastily retrieved them from the fridge, put both hands in the dough, and licked them clean while Nash manhandled the butter. The kitchen, if it could still be called that after so much abuse, now looked like some sort of flour-covered battlefield, and it would take her five times as long to clean up what she could easily have done solo. Her patience was gone, as was her willingness to ever bake with her children again. Really, what had she been thinking?

"Well, this is something."

Suddenly Gaines stood in the kitchen, appearing through the mist. Or in this case a spray of flour from Charlotte's latest over-enthusiastic cup dumping. Jordan was so startled she tossed the egg she'd been about to crack into the air and Gaines, being Gaines, casually reached over her head and caught it mid-air, keeping it perfectly intact. Then he opened his palm and presented it to her like a freshly picked gardenia.

Instead of taking it Jordan remained staring at him, speechless with surprise at his unexpected appearance.

"You said to let myself in," he reminded her, smiling a bit devilishly at her confoundment.

"I did at that," Jordan agreed, suddenly aware of all the twelve thousand hairs that had escaped her messy bun and were now covered in flour and plastered to her face. In contrast he was impeccable, as ever. "You look…" her words trailed away, unable to continue under their own steam, all at once realizing they were being fueled by awkwardness and it was better to stop before they slammed into the wall of humiliation. Any number of words could have filled in the blank, but "delectable" hovered on the tip of her tongue, and that would never do. "Serviceable," she finally blurted, hoping he failed to notice the newly acquired sheen of panic sweat on her upper lip.

One corner of his mouth tipped, roguishly, she thought. "I am always happy to be of service," he agreed and though he had probably meant it innocently, Jordan flushed and looked away, unable to maintain eye contact. What on earth was going on? Why did Gaines seem to be flirting with her? Was it merely his default mode and she, newly single, had been sucked into the flirtation radius? He must have some sort of gravitational pull on single women, which she now was, that left them flustered and discombobulated by his overabundance of charm. It bothered her, that. Both his flirtation and her reaction to it. Because he had to know how vulnerable and lonely she was. As such, it seemed cruel to play on that, to rely on their long friendship as a buffer, certain she could use it to resist him. Similarly, it bothered her that she couldn't seem to muster her usual protection.

Then men in Jay's world, men like Gaines, rode their charm, good looks, and high levels of testosterone like a team of Pony Express horses. Only they seemed to know the password to make it stop; everyone else was haplessly in danger of being run over. Jordan had always been impervious. While married to Jay, safe and boy-next-door cute Jay, she had watched their antics with high amusement, witnessed dozens upon dozens of women get caught up in the myth—*a Navy SEAL*—only to get tossed away at some unfortunate point. Jordan had shaken her head, not only at the dangerous and borderline cruel game the men played, but at the woman's willingness to go along. Really, had they no respect? Were they so easily swayed by a square jaw and daunting military career?

Apparently yes, and now she was one of them.

Gaines helped himself to the drawer with the dishcloths. Jordan watched while he wetted it with warm water and then, instead of attacking any of the counters or cabinets that had been covered in today's baking war, turned his attention to her, tenderly wiping her cheeks, eyes, forehead, and chin as his free hand held her still. His eyes followed the movements of his cloth, intent and precise, giving careful attention to detail so Jordan was suddenly left wishing she'd remembered to apply makeup that morning. Not that it would matter now when he was washing her.

Finally satisfied, he paused cleaning and smiled, his left hand now cupping her neck as his forearm rested on her shoulder. "Hey."

"Hey," she repeated, soft and a little shy. "Sorry it's so...and I'm so...and everything is so..." She faltered, not wanting to point out her ineptness, in case he hadn't noticed, but also needing to address her ineptness, because of course he'd noticed.

"What are you talking about?" he asked, smiling deeper so his hide and seek dimple popped.

"I just..." apparently they were feigning ignorance over the ineptness. Duly noted and moving on. "So, you're here."

"Is that okay?" he asked. His thumb began smoothing up and down her windpipe and her brain faltered and short circuited.

"What?"

"Is that okay?" Gaines repeated, only Jordan had lost the thread of the original conversation and now thought he was asking if it was okay that his thumb eased up and down her windpipe.

"Yes, that's, um, good, really good thumb work."

Now his other dimple popped. "What?"

Suddenly Jordan remembered the original question and wanted to crawl in a dark hole until the humiliation passed. *Divert, divert, divert.* "Are you hungry? You must be hungry."

"Starved," Gaines said, but he didn't let go or look away and the way he was looking at her was sort of...wolfish? She'd only ever received that look from Jay, when he came home from deployment or assignment, high on testosterone and intent on "claiming his marital right," as he used to jokingly declare. But surely she had it wrong and Gaines wasn't now giving her the same look. This must be part of his spiel, the one he used on unsuspecting women. He was likely so used to the routine he didn't even realize he was wasting it on Jordan. And of course it was a waste because...because why? All of a sudden she couldn't seem to remember. It was one of those tunnel sorts of moments, when everything faded to background and there was only her and Gaines, his hand warm and possessive on her neck. Jordan had just started to tip the slightest bit forward on her toes when Nash launched a wooden spoon at her, bashing it hard against her shin.

She howled, hopping on one foot with the pain of it, and her masochistic baby giggled maniacally, taking another swing to try and elicit a similar response on the other shin. Thankfully Gaines kicked into gear once again with the reflexes and saved her aching legs, swooping the baby into his grasp and relinquishing him of the spoon in one smooth motion.

"Okay?" he asked Jordan, though he couldn't disguise his own amusement.

She nodded, blinking back tears.

"This little guy's got quite the arm," he said, bouncing Nash who trilled out a loud yell, enjoying the shift in his voice with every volley.

Jordan didn't reply because, as much as the smack had stung her leg, the tears had nothing to do with Nash and everything to do with Gaines. And also herself. What was he doing, flirting with her that way? And what was she doing, responding to him? If Nash hadn't stopped her, what might have happened? Was she about to throw herself at Gaines and kiss him?

Mortifying, absolutely mortifying. *He would have been forced to reject you; you would have made him feel terrible, might have wrecked everything between you. Don't be so stupid, Jordan. Don't be so relentlessly stupid. And also desperate. Needy. Clingy. Crazy, and everything else you've heard the guys called their SEAL groupies over the years. You're not one of them, not one of the desperate and lonely hangers on. You're a recent widow with class and dignity. Act like it!*

Nash, tired of the bouncing, began to squirm. Gaines set him down and he was off, ready to find more trouble. "Hey," Gaines said, easing his arm around Jordan who still stood on one foot like a flamingo. He gave her shoulders a bracing squeeze. "That hurt."

His tone was a mix of laughter and sympathy but Jordan, so hungry for the sympathy she felt like she was starving, leaned in and pressed her nose to the crook of his neck. His head tilted, resting comfortingly on hers as his grip tightened. Her foot lowered and she took a deep breath, inhaling the distinct scent of him, one she didn't know she'd catalogued and assigned until that moment.

I know exactly how Gaines smells. My body knows and remembers, she realized. She squeezed her eyes shut and clutched his shirt in her fists, suddenly feeling like maybe class and dignity were overrated. Because this, this feeling in this moment, of belonging and security and comfort and care, were far more valuable currency, more potent than anything she'd previously encountered.

Gaines ran a hand down the back of her head, curving it against her skull in a gesture that, unless she was misreading it, felt possessive. Slowly his face slid sideways, beard rasping on her forehead until his soft lips slid against the fragile skin below her hairline. His lips began to part, with a kiss or a word she had no idea because at that moment a furry nose popped between them, creating a space like a crowbar as first Charlotte's stuffed dog and then Charlotte herself wedged between them.

"Wibs wants a hug, too," she demanded, holding her stuffed dog aloft for Gaines's inspection.

Gaines took a step back and regarded her with a smile. "Absolutely." When he picked her up and held her tightly, Jordan's heart pinched painfully. She missed Jay, yearned for the way he'd do the same. But it was also right somehow that Gaines was here, doing it in his stead because Gaines had always been there, had always loved on her kids. It wasn't new or unusual, but she still felt the lack of their father. It was a strange mix of pleasure and disappointment. Gaines was here, and that was wonderful; Jay was not, and that was horrible. Somehow it was possible to feel both things and she stared at the picture Charlotte and Gaines presented, wondering what other things it was possible to feel together. Grief…but also love?

Jordan jumped as if she'd been stung, and that was how she felt. Of course she wasn't in love with Gaines. *My lands,* she thought, pressing her hand against her cheek as she turned her attention away from the beautiful picture her friend and daughter presented. She was lonely and desperate for comfort and she could not, absolutely would not mistake that for something more. Not for anyone.

It's not for anyone, though. It's for Gaines, her sneaky brain told her.

It wasn't as if she'd felt any sort of attraction to Ridge, Ethan, Frog, or Jones. Or any other man. Perhaps it was merely proximity. Gaines was nearby, and no one else was.

She let herself believe it, but as Gaines stormed through the house, making Charlotte giggle as he pretended he'd forgotten she was there and still attached, she knew it was a lie. The truth, however, was still too fraught to handle, and she refused to let herself find it.

CHAPTER 17

Maybe it was all the new thoughts and feelings jangling inside her that caused the dream. Maybe the dream was her mind's way of trying to parse fact from feeling. Whatever the reason it was one of those gripping dreams, the kind that clutches the dreamer by the throat with unnamed dread and tension and won't let go.

First it was Jay, lying gently and peacefully beside her. They both slept, and then Jordan woke. She rolled over and looked down at him, and when he opened his eyes and smiled up at her, it was Gaines. She froze with panic, and then he reached for her, grasping her hips and pulling her snugly beside him. His head dipped, his lips almost on hers, but instead of kissing her he whispered.

There's someone in this room.

Jordan's eyes popped open. She stilled her breathing and froze as the dream mingled with reality. Was someone in the room or was that part of her overheated imagination?

With something akin to horror she peeled open her eyes and made herself look. No one was in her room. She was alone. Relieved, she sat up, her eyes landing on the empty space beside her with a jumble of relief and disappointment. And more than a little yearning. Whether the yearning was for Jay or Gaines seemed to be the source of her confusion. She was about to lie back down when she heard it, the tiny clatter of something amiss. A noise that made her wish she had a cat so she could blame its midnight ramblings. There was no cat, however, and no way to easily dismiss the noise, the tiny squeak of someone taking a step in the living room.

Maybe Gaines decided to sneak in and make certain everything was okay.

It was the type of thing he would do, she knew, show up unexpectedly for a perimeter sweep to settle his own mind about her safety. But somehow she also knew that if Gaines did such a thing, Jordan would never know because he wouldn't make a sound. He was, after all, a spy.

If not for the children, Jordan would be content to pull the blanket over her head and feign ignorance. To hope and pray the sound was nothing and would soon go away. But with her babies nearby and unprotected, it was up to her to track the source of that sound. Grabbing her phone, she debated a split second what to do. What if she contacted Gaines—again—got him out of bed—again—dragged him over here in the middle of the night—again—for another wild goose chase—again. She couldn't. Wouldn't. Gaines was exhausted and he needed his sleep, if not more than she did. He was, after all, a spy with an important job that often made him miss large chunks of sleep and rest.

As a compromise to both of them, she typed in the text but waited to send it.

I heard a noise. Checking it out. Come if you get this text.

There. If and when it turned out to once again be her overheated imagination, she would delete the text. But if, on the itty-bitty chance it was an actual intruder, she'd have a rescue ready. Gaines would, she knew, move heaven and earth to get there in a fast amount of time. All the more reason not to text him yet. If he became injured speeding to her aid, she'd never forgive herself. Even if his daily life put him in much worse danger, Jordan would hold herself accountable if something happened to him on her watch.

Phone in hand, she crept from her room, allowing her eyes to adjust to the dimness of the house. She didn't do nightlights, after reading a pediatrician's stance on the increased risk for nearsightedness in children. But now she regretted the lack. The only light in her dim abode came from a few clocks and electronics, not nearly enough to make out shapes. Unless they moved. *Please don't let them move,* she silently prayed, taking a step outside her room, forcing herself to be brave by virtue of being a mother.

Thoughts of the kids fueled her steps. This time she would do it right; she would neutralize the threat before securing the assets. Or something less menacing. *Make sure the kids are safe.* That was all this was. She was satisfying her overheated imagination to make certain her children were safe.

As she meandered through the house, she began to calm. Nothing was amiss, nothing was out of place. No one moved, no more noises made her suspicious. Her breathing had almost returned to normal by the time she checked Nash, careful not to make a sound. If he saw, heard, or even smelled her he would wake, wanting to nurse. And she, naïve though she may be, still held on to some hope of weaning him soon.

Nash didn't stir. Jordan eased out of his room and closed the door with no noise. She intended to turn toward Charlotte's room, but before she could do so the little girl let out an ear-splitting wail. Sprinting now, Jordan reached her room and threw open the door, taking everything in with a primal mix of panic and protection. If someone was hurting her baby, he'd soon wish he'd never been born.

There was nothing and no one, though. As with the rest of the house the room was undisturbed, save for the little girl now sitting on her knees and weeping loudly. Satisfied there was no threat, Jordan sat on the bed and attempted to soothe, but Charlotte pushed her away.

"Wibs," Charlotte pled, over and over. "I want Wibs."

Jordan searched for the dog, tipping sideways over the bed to find that he'd fallen or been pushed aside. She settled the animal within Charlotte's grasp, but that didn't stop her sobbing.

"No, I want Wibs. Uncle Wibs, the weal one," Charlotte insisted, now clutching the stuffed dog and using him to dry her tears.

Jordan attempted to calm her on her own a few more times, to no avail. Then she attempted reason, something pointless on a three year old who wasn't inconsolable. "Honey, Uncle Ribs is in his own house. He's sleeping."

"I NEED HIM," Charlotte insisted, becoming impossibly more unmanageable.

Jordan wrung her hands, staring helplessly at the door. She had never seen Charlotte this upset, had never been unable to calm her before. Was it an effect of Jay's death? At long last did Charlotte put a name to what had been amiss? Was calling for Ribs her way of grieving for Jay?

Whatever the reason, there seemed to be no end in sight. Eventually the sound would wake Nash and then she'd really be in trouble. There had only been a few combined meltdowns since Nash was born, but they had been enough to drive Jordan to the edge of sanity.

Grasping her phone, she erased the text to Gaines and called him instead.

"Jordy," he declared in the half-alert mumble she'd come to associate with his disturbed sleep. It wasn't the same as her incoherent midnight rambling. Instead his was ready to defend and protect, probably already included him rolling out of bed and reaching for pants. *Don't think about his pants.* "What's going on?"

He had to hear Charlotte in the background. Jordan had to almost yell to be heard. "Charlotte is having a meltdown. She wants you and I..." *And I want you, too.* "I know it's the middle of the night and you have work and..."

"Jordy," he interrupted, urging her to spit it out.

She took a breath. "Can you come?"

"I'm on my way," he said. In the background she heard a car start and smiled. Somehow the knowledge that he would have come even before she asked was almost as comforting as his actual presence, or so she thought until, almost an impossible time later, he eased into the room and swept Charlotte into his arms.

It only took a few swipes of his hand and a couple of reassuring kisses before she stopped crying and melted into him, pressing her tear-streaked little face into his shoulder. He let her shudders and snuffles die down to a reasonable level before trying to make her talk. Eventually he asked a question.

"What's wrong with my baby?" His tone was tender, as was his touch, middle finger stroking her forehead, pushing the wet hair off her cheeks. "Why are you so upset?"

Her tiny fists tangled in his shirt, holding tight. "I don't want him," she murmured, so softly they had to lean in to hear it.

Gaines looked at Jordan but she shrugged. Later she would tell him her theory about this being because of Jay's death, but she didn't want to bring it up when Charlotte was beginning to calm. Already her eyes were drooping.

"Who, baby?" Gaines whispered, angling her toward the bed in an attempt to ease her back under the covers.

"The man," Charlotte insisted, voice growing softer with renewed sleep.

"What man?" Jordan asked because Gaines was now shuffling her further into the bed, righting the covers around her.

The movement came to a standstill, as did their hearts, when Charlotte sleepily mumbled. "The man who stands over my bed."

🜚

They stared at each other, blinking in confusion over Charlotte's inert form. After a considerable time, and accompanied by her snores, Gaines eased his arm from beneath her and tiptoed out of the room behind Jordan.

By unspoken agreement, Gaines would do a perimeter check. Jordan meandered to her bedroom to wait, too distracted to ponder her choice of location. She intended to perch on the edge of the bed, but evidence of her disturbed slumber proved too inviting. She eased into the tousled bed, paddling her feet contentedly. Cool sheets were a small luxury, and one she'd gladly accept.

Gaines joined her shortly, kicking off his shoes before stretching out on top of the covers. It was odd, she thought, how natural it felt to have him there. As if neither of them gave it a thought. Of course she and the gorgeous spy would confer in her bed. Where else?

Gaines reached out and touched a finger to her cheek, alerting her to the fact that he was on to her wry amusement. And now he smiled in response. The moment stretched, erasing the earlier stress.

"Find anything?" she asked, already knowing the answer. He would have led with it, if he had. She rolled toward him, tucking her hand under her cheek.

"Nope." He rolled toward her, mimicking her pose. The bed was king size, and yet they were at the center of it, very close together.

"I heard a noise," she confessed in a near whisper, unwilling to disturb the peace. "It woke me."

He frowned. "What sort of noise?"

She thought back, trying and failing to place it. "I don't know. Something that didn't belong." She recounted checking the house. His scowl deepened.

"You should have called me then."

"I didn't want to distu…" she began, but he pressed a finger gently to her lips, cutting off the word.

"Never, ever, ever would you disturb me. I want to know. Every time, every noise."

She couldn't respond because his finger was still on her mouth, a strangely intimate thing, to have someone touch your mouth. She swallowed hard and he did the same, removing his finger and curling it back into his palm.

"I should…" he began, but didn't know how to continue. Neither of them knew what to do with the unprecedented situation.

Jordan reached out and gave his button-down shirt a little tug, settling the matter without addressing any of the odd tension. "You can't sleep in this."

He sat up, eyeing her as he reached for the hem and paused. All of a sudden she realized the problem. Gaines, perfect specimen he was, was self-conscious over his scar.

"Gaines," she said, a bit reproachful. She'd seen him shirtless a dozen times; she didn't care.

With a resigned sigh, he peeled off the shirt and tossed it aside, lying down, shoulders a tiny bit stiff as if bracing for something unpleasant.

Jordan stared at his namesake unabashed, newly fascinated. There was a lot about her husband and his friends she didn't know, secrets they would take to their graves. They were cagey about their handles. To this day Jordan had no idea why her husband was called Shimmer. Jay had been tight-lipped about it, as was everyone else. But she did know how Ribs got his name. It was the entire reason for his handle, a jagged scar that ran the length of his ribcage. The remnant of a bite from a massive shark, a mission gone horribly wrong. Her finger reached out and eased over each jagged edge, tracing the outline the shark left behind. Gaines sucked a breath, muscles rippling beneath her touch. Absently she wondered if he was ticklish, but in the moment she was too intent.

"I remember this," she whispered. Not the actual shark attack, of course. She hadn't been present for the event. But she'd been there for the aftermath, witnessed how shaken Jay and all the guys were when they returned home, even though they'd tried to hide it, to keep going and pretend nothing was amiss. She had no idea about the others, but Jay's nightmares had lasted for months. One night four months later he'd woken in tears and panic, clinging to her.

We almost lost him, Jordy. You have no idea how close it was. He almost bled out in my arms. If not for Ridge and the tourniquet... He either couldn't or wouldn't say more about what happened, but it had been enough of a glimpse to allow part of his horror to leach onto her. She had clung in return, soothing him as she shed her own tears.

Jordan swallowed a sudden lump, remembering anew. Life without Gaines was impossible to fathom. Somehow he'd always been there, hovering in the background of her life with Jay.

"You could have died," she whispered, finger trailing the outline, all the way up before going back down again.

"Lots of times," Gaines returned, watching her intently.

"Not the reassurance I was aiming for," she said.

"Why do you need it?" he croaked, his voice a hoarse whisper.

Her hand froze. Their eyes caught and held. She could have pawned him off, taken a dive, said something glib and offhand. *We're friends; of course I don't want anything to happen to you.*

Instead she said, "I don't know."

He weighed that a few beats then, satisfied, reached out and took her hand, winding their fingers together. "Okay." He brought her knuckles to his mouth and kissed them before resting their combined hands on his chest and closing his eyes.

After a few more sleepy blinks, Jordan fell asleep, her hand still nestled in Gaines's cozy embrace.

In the morning Gaines woke to the feeling that someone was watching him. He lay on his stomach and Jordan, as he'd predicted, was on her back, staring ponderously at him. He thought perhaps she was having regrets over their impromptu sleepover, but then she spoke and dispelled that notion.

"How are you?" she asked, tone sincere and full of concern for his wellbeing.

He smiled because she had no idea, none whatsoever, how long he'd dreamed of this exact moment. In his life, few dreams lived up to the hype. There was a reason Confucius said to be careful what you wished for. The reality never seemed to turn out like the vision. But this, this moment, this feeling, this unnamed thing that was happening between him and Jordan—the fruition of a secret dream he'd cherished for thirteen years—was somehow impossibly better. He wondered why that was. Right now it was too early to figure it out.

"I'm good," he said, an understatement. Ten thousand possibilities ran through his mind, every one of them wrong and inappropriate, given her fragility. She was a bubble of temptation in tiny shorts and a pre-pregnancy t-shirt, one that hadn't stretched enough to fit her new, maternal body. He caught an enticing snippet of skin on her stomach and, not being a choirboy, reached over to stroke it with his thumb.

Maybe Jordan faced a bit of her own temptation because her hand reached out and smoothed along his shoulder, finger tracing his muscles. "Are your cuddle needs being met?"

He shook his head.

Her brows rose. "No?"

"Now you know my secret shame, Jordy; I'm a snuggle pit. An endless chasm of cuddle void."

She giggled, her tummy moving under his fingertips. Gaines smiled harder, so hard he felt like his cheeks stretched.

"Gaines," she said.

"Mm."

"I like this."

"Jordy."

"Mm."

"Me too."

The bedroom door opened. They saw no one until Nash's head popped over the side of the bed. He scrambled up, pulling himself with fists held in blanket, an ace climber, until he reached Jordan. As before he had no qualms about claiming his breakfast. Unlike previously Jordan was awake enough to be discreet in her arrangement. The intimacy of the moment only added to the spell now weaving around them. Gaines reached out and sleeked his fingers over Nash's fine baby hair, his heart tumbling when Nash grasped his finger and gave it a squeeze.

The moment felt impossibly beautiful, and then somehow it got better when Charlotte padded into the room, climbed up on Gaines's side of the bed, and shimmied down between them. Gaines kissed the top of her head and she nestled against him with renewed drowsiness.

"Gaines," Jordan whispered.

"Hmm," he replied.

"I like this even better."

It had never occurred to Gaines that he might love someone's kids as well as he loved hers, until it happened. "Same, Jordy, same."

They shared a smile over the kids' heads. Jordan reached out a few fingers. He grasped them and gave them a squeeze and somehow that tiny touch was more potent than anything that came before.

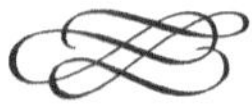

"I'm not going to lie; you don't look good."

"Thanks." Ribs swiped a weary hand over his stubbled face as Ridge made his keen-eyed inspection. "Stayed the night at Jordan's again."

Ridge's brows rose slightly. "I didn't get an alert from the locals. Unless it was a personal matter?"

Ribs paused mid-yawn to regard him with disdain. "Would I be here if it were?"

"Good point," Ridge said. Relaxed now, he slid a platter of muffins between them, his wife's influence. Pre-Maggie, Ridge would have continued to work while Ribs poured out his heart. Now he took exactly one quarter of a muffin—his only concession to sugar—and sat back, waiting patiently.

"Man, you guys and your wives," Ribs observed, reaching for the three quarters of muffin Ridge left behind. "I can't get over it."

"Neither can we," Ridge agreed, chewing thoughtfully. "After years of puzzling it over, I still can't figure out why it happens this way."

"You mean why you're so much better now?" Ribs prodded.

Ridge nodded, unprovoked. "The only thing I can come up with is that this is how it's supposed to be. Remaining alone and untethered is unnatural and, eventually, leads to ruin."

"Comforting, thanks," Ribs said.

Ridge's eloquent brow rose again. "Are you untethered, though? Are you really?"

Ribs took a breath to answer and let it out, deflated. "I don't know. I don't know anything anymore."

"Did you ever?" Ridge asked.

"I thought I used to. I thought Shimmer did, too."

The levity died away as they both stared at the plate of muffins, mourning their fallen friend. Ridge took a deep breath. "Right, so what brings you?"

"This thing with Jordan."

"You mean how you're in love with her and she has no idea?" Ridge said.

"No."

"You mean how she's your best friend's widow and you don't know if she's ready?" Ridge tried.

"No."

"You mean…"

"Maybe I could tell you instead of you trying to guess," Ribs groused.

"This is the most fun I've had in a while," Ridge returned. "But go ahead."

"Have there been any developments on Shimmer's suicide?" Surely Ridge would have told him if he'd found anything, but given the recent events, he needed to ask.

"Ethan's been on it. And he's been…detailed." It was probably an understatement. If Ethan had a personal stake in the game, which he did, then he would be ruthless in his search for answers. "But so far nothing has come up. Each way we come at it, it keeps looking like what we first believed."

They stared at the muffins again, once again coming to terms that their friend, whom they'd both loved, had chosen to end things forever.

"I assume there's a reason you're asking," Ridge said at last, shifting them away from the uncomfortable silence.

Ribs told him about Charlotte's proclamation, the weird noises that had been waking Jordan. In return Ridge gave him the hard stare, the one that said he was puzzling something and frustrated because he was unable to find the answer. Ribs knew the feeling because he felt the same.

"Jordan's not making it up," he summarized, somewhat defensively.

"I never believed she was," Ridge returned agreeably.

"But there's nothing. I've swept that perimeter so hard the spiders moved away to get some peace. There is *nothing*. Not one trace. Whoever he is, the guy is good. But if he's not connected to Shimmer, I don't know what to think."

"It's possible it's connected to Shimmer, but not his death," Ridge suggested. There were always people with vendettas in their world. Some took longer to come to fruition.

Ribs mashed a crumb on the desk, staring at his finger to avoid looking at Ridge. "It's different when it's personal."

"Yes."

"I don't know how to do it."

"The same. Compartmentalize. Keep the job the job, deal with the other stuff later, when it's over."

Ribs blew out a breath. He tried to imagine compartmentalizing Jordan and the kids, shoving them into a corner of his heart and focusing on the job, but all he could remember was Charlotte's face pressed to his chest, her baby fists clinging. Jordan's soft and small hand between his bigger ones, Nash's glee at evading capture and causing mayhem.

Ridge knocked on the desk between them, startling him. "When the time comes you'll do it. Because you have to. It's the only way to keep them safe."

It seemed so long ago now that Maggie had been in the crosshairs, when Ridge had led the rescue to save her. He might like to pretend he'd been completely closed off, but none of them had ever seen him so rattled, so intent. That was how they knew, long before he said the words, that Maggie was the one who would remain when the mission was over. Even if some emotion had leaked through, he'd found a way. Ribs would, too. He gave a small nod of assent. Ridge made a flicking motion toward the door, albeit a friendly one. Ridge might be a task-oriented super boss, but he was always available when they needed him. What surprised Ribs was how much they continued to need him. None of them were boys anymore, and yet the dynamic remained with Ridge as their forever mentor.

Ribs paused and turned back. Ridge's brows rose in question again. "I really love and appreciate you, I hope you know." After Shimmer, it felt like he needed to say it more, to make certain the people in his world heard all the things they needed to hear.

"I do, and same," Ridge replied. Then he repeated the flicking motion toward the door. This time Ribs took it, closing the door softly behind him as he made his exit.

CHAPTER 19

Jordan knew she must be crazy, to plan a birthday party in the midst of so much grief and chaos. But this was the first year Charlotte had an awareness and understanding of her birthday, of what it meant to have a party. Jordan didn't have the heart to disillusion her, not after everything else. But there were a lot of logistical concerns.

First of all she had no idea who to invite. Her mother would be on a cruise. Jay's parents made it clear they couldn't make it. Their tone, when she asked, had felt disapproving, as if they thought she shouldn't host a party when the grief was so raw. But maybe that was her own sensitivity over the matter.

Charlotte wasn't in school, so there were no little friends to have over. It felt too needy and aggressive to invite the near-strangers from the library's story time, especially after the debacle of a play date with Blarney and Clipper.

In the end she decided she was overthinking it. Charlotte might have a vague notion of what a party entailed—people and presents and cake—but she didn't know those people were supposed to be her age. It would be enough to have guests there to pay attention to her and give them a reason to eat party food. So after a brief few days of agony, wherein Jordan tried to assemble a list of Charlotte's pint-sized social group, she instead scratched that idea and decided to invite her own friends, hers and Jay's. Once that was decided, she began to relax. Amelia and Ethan and Ridge and Maggie had already RSVP'd. Frog and his wife were on the fence, pending her family's visit. And then there was Ribs.

Her stomach did the flippy thing it had been doing whenever she thought of him lately. As if someone had broken in and released a fresh wave of butterflies. She didn't like it, but she also couldn't seem to undo it.

Face the facts, kid. You have a crush on Gaines. It was so mortifying she almost couldn't stand it. Six weeks a widow and see how low she'd sunk. Instead of healing she'd developed an unhealthy and unrequited crush on her husband's best friend. She felt confused and ashamed by the unwarranted feelings, but mostly embarrassed that she'd become such a sad cliché.

On the other hand she had no idea how she could help it, not with Gaines being so solicitous and tender and concerned and *there*. He'd shown up in the last six weeks more than Jay had in the last three years.

She gasped at the disloyal thought and pressed her hand to her eyes, almost drowning in guilt. How could she think such things about the man she'd been married to for twelve years? On the other hand, how could she not?

The fact was that she and Jay had some serious problems. His death and her grief didn't change that. As much as she didn't want to be easy pickings for the first man who paid her a bit of attention, neither did she want to memorialize Jay, to make him a saint when he hadn't been. They'd loved each other, but life hadn't been perfect.

"Not to nitpick, but this would go a lot better if you'd stop throwing your hands over your face," Amelia said.

Jordan lowered her hands and stared at her stylist and friend in the mirror. "Oh, I forgot you were there."

"I get that a lot," Amelia said, a lie. She was usually impossible to ignore, beautiful and witty, the sort of woman who lit up a room and made heads turn. If Jordan didn't love her so much, she'd probably resent her. "Are you thinking of the kids? I'm positive they're okay." Amelia usually did Jordan's hair at her house so the kids could roam free. Today Jordan came to the salon and her children, at Amelia's suggestion, were with her brother, Darren, and his stepdaughter, McKenna.

"Actually, no," Jordan admitted.

"Good, because he has a lot of faults, a *lot*, but Darren is freakishly good with kids. It's kind of a Pied Piper situation. Kids flock to him. And I think McKenna and Charlotte will hit it off."

Jordan smiled at her in the mirror. It was nice to have a friend who thought about your kid enough to try and find her a friend. "I'm sure they will," Jordan agreed. She'd met Darren a couple of times before, along with Babs, and felt no qualms about leaving her kids with him. Strange since she left them so rarely, but Darren was that kind of guy—good and upstanding and conscientious. And it was only for an hour and a half. After the first thirty minutes Babs would arrive home from work. Jordan had promised to return the favor next week and host McKenna so the newlyweds could have a date, a favorable arrangement for both of them. She made a mental note to invite them to Charlotte's party, squirming under Amelia's intense inspection.

"If it's not the kids, then it must be…" Amelia let the words hang.

"World peace?" Jordan said weakly.

"Or a certain peacekeeper," Amelia said, wagging her brows.

Jordan hadn't mentioned a word about Gaines to her, but somehow she knew, proving that she must be completely obvious in her newfound crush. She felt her cheeks go crimson.

"Stop blushing, you're throwing off my mojo," Amelia groused, frowning as she gave Jordan's hair a little tug. "Why are you blushing, anyway?"

"Because it's so completely humiliating," Jordan said.

"Which part?" Amelia asked.

"All of it. The fact that I'm a recent widow with a crush. The fact that I'm one of them now."

"Normal human female?" Amelia guessed.

"No, one of the groupies. I mean seriously. How many times have we thrown shade at them, tossed them our disdain for obsessing over a guy merely because he's a SEAL, because he's handsome and manly and wears a uniform."

Amelia scowled at her in the mirror, set aside her scissors, rested her hands on Jordan's shoulders, and gave her a stern look in the mirror. "Jordan, I say this with all the love in my heart: you're a moron."

"That's what I've been trying to tell you," Jordan said, tossing her hands in frustration.

"Listen, you dope, you're not a SEAL groupie. You were a SEAL wife. And you're not having feelings because a guy is handsome and wears a uniform; you're having feelings because he's been your friend for more than a decade and he's stepped up in a major way."

Jordan blinked at her, letting the words settle over her. "Oh," she drawled, multiple epiphanies dawning. "What about the part where I'm a recent widow?"

"No, that part is still bad," Amelia said, picking up her scissors and pointing them accusingly at Jordan in the mirror.

Jordan couldn't help it, she snorted a laugh that was quickly followed by another and then another and then, ten minutes later, they were still bent over laughing and wiping tears.

"I'm such a mess," Jordan declared, wiping her nose.

"Yep, but so is he. So is everybody," Amelia agreed, picking up another stalk of hair to trim. "Life is messy. It comes hard and fast. Grab on to the good parts and don't let go."

"Everything magically makes sense when I'm sitting in this chair," Jordan mused.

"I'm not sure if it's because I have a lot of wisdom or we're always high on salon fumes," Amelia said, causing them to start on another round of giggles that couldn't be stopped until the door jangled. Amelia's husband, Ethan, entered, followed by Gaines. Both men smiled as they approached. Ethan paused to kiss his wife while Gaines crossed his arms and regarded Jordan in the mirror.

"This is where the magic happens," she told him.

"Impossible," he replied.

"That Amelia can do something with all this?" she motioned to her hair and face.

"No, that Amelia could be the cause of the magic when I know for a fact it's been happening at least the past thirteen years."

In the mirror, Amelia and Ethan exchanged a surreptitious fist bump.

"Do you routinely drop by beauty salons to say smooth things to lonely widows?" Jordan asked.

"Not as often as I'd like," he said. "I'm here to pick you up."

"I drove."

"Not a literal pickup. The sort where I take you and the children to supper and then…"

Her brows rose. "And then?"

He shrugged, tossing her a half smile. "We'll see where it goes."

Amelia and Ethan exchanged another fist bump.

"You know we can see you," Jordan told them.

"And we can hear you. That's why we're doing this," Ethan returned. "My man is doing well. Don't ruin this for him."

"He could be doing better," Amelia inserted.

"How?" Ribs asked her.

She tipped forward to whisper in his ear.

"I'll take that under advisement," he said, nodding.

"Oh, my goodness, you guys. Our friendship has crossed too many lines today," Jordan said, pressing a hand to her overheated cheek.

"Ours?" Ethan said, motioning around the group. "Or yours?" This time the motion only included Jordan and Ribs.

"I…" Jordan stopped short when she realized they were all staring at her, genuinely awaiting an answer. "I have to go get my children," she resolved, aiming for primness.

"I think that's my cue to provide a rescue," Ribs said, extending his hand to help her up. When their fingers touched, Jordan felt a tingle that went all the way down to her toes. And when she stood he didn't release her. Instead he tucked her hand in his, leading her alongside him toward the street.

Jordan glanced helplessly behind her, in time to see Amelia and Ethan exchange one final fist bump, followed by a kiss.

CHAPTER 20

Gaines still had hold of her hand. He used it to lead her to the passenger door of her car. Jay and his friends weren't really the sort of men to let a woman drive them places. Jordan supposed she should take a stand for her independence, but really she didn't care. She had never acclimated to heavy and aggressive DC traffic. In fact she had missed Jay shuttling her places and was almost ridiculously grateful for the time away from the wheel.

"So, Miss Jordan," Gaines began as soon as he'd pulled away from the curb.

"Yes, Mister Gaines," she returned, using the opportunity to stare at his perfect profile. Straight nose, full lips, long lashes, stubbled cheeks. A little part of her brain hoped it would be a longer than usual drive so she could keep staring at the literal eye candy beside her. Parts of her brain she previously didn't know existed were lighting up, like she was sitting next to a Da Vinci while listening to Mozart and doing Sudoku.

"I would like an answer to a question, please."

"And what is the question?" she returned.

"Why is it when I try to tell you you're beautiful you become flustered and want to argue with me?" He darted her a glance and she faced quickly forward, immediately flustered and defensive.

"I don't."

"You do."

"I don't know what you're talking about," she insisted.

"Just now, at Amelia's salon."

She waved her hand dismissively. "That was you being you. Of course I can't respond to it."

He waited until he paused at a stop sign to look at her. "What? What does any of that mean?"

"You know how it is, Gaines."

"Really, really no." The car behind him beeped. Reluctantly he forced his attention away from her and began to drive. "Please explain."

She was helpless to understand the annoyance in his tone when it was all so obvious to her. She needed to do this the right way, so she wouldn't cause offense. She drew a deep breath. "For thirteen years I've been on the periphery of your life, Jay's life, the team's life. I've gotten an up close glimpse at how your world works, how the game is played. I know how it goes."

"Jordy, I don't understand a word coming out of your mouth."

"I'm saying I've lost track of the number of women and girls who have come and gone in that time. I grew up in a navy town, and I always, *always* understood how it was."

"How what was?" he asked, exasperated.

"The game, the thing you all do. There's an overabundance of testosterone involved; it has to find an outlet. A sort of pressure release valve. One of those happens to be picking up women. I was miraculously lucky to find a guy who didn't do that. I don't expect to find lightning in a bottle twice in a lifetime." She turned her gaze out the window, missing the raw and wounded look Gaines tossed her way.

The rest of the drive was quiet. Jordan remained unwitting that she'd plunged them both into sadness, her remembering her past, Gaines thinking of their future. He parked in Darren's drive and turned off the car. Jordan started to get out, but he put out a hand, halting her.

"In the past thirteen years, how many women have I dated?" he asked.

She bit her lip, thinking. "Three I've met."

"Three," he repeated.

She blinked at him. "What?"

"Not three you've met, three women. Total. I'm not that guy, Jordan, not the sort who uses women and tosses them away. And it makes me so sad that you who should know me so well think differently."

All of a sudden she realized she'd hurt his feelings and tears sprang to her eyes because it was the last thing in the world she wanted. "Gaines, I'm sorry," she said sincerely, resting her hand on his arm. "I guess I am guilty of lumping you in with the others. And Jay used to tell me stories, nameless faceless stories of some of the antics that went on. I assumed he was talking about you."

He shook his head slowly back and forth.

She glanced down at her hand, still resting on his arm. "Why only three?"

"What?"

She looked up again, meeting his eyes, eyes that now bounced cagily away. If she didn't know better, she'd say the question made him nervous, but she couldn't figure out why. "Why only three women? In all that time. Why so few?"

"Because..." he started and stopped, beautiful mouth hanging slightly ajar. "Because I...because..."

Her heart kicked into overdrive, though she had no idea why. Gently, her hand smoothed back and forth on his arm. He stared at it a few beats, composing himself. At last he took a deep breath.

"Jordan, I guess what I want you to know is that when I tell you something from this point forward, I'm not feeding you a line. I'm being sincere. I would never lie to you." Tentatively his hand eased out, covering hers.

Now it was her turn to stare at their combined hands. "Gaines, you know I was twenty when Jay and I got married. We were married for twelve years. I've been a widow six weeks. I guess what I'm trying to say is that I don't have a lot experience in my current position as a single woman. I'm sorry I hurt your feelings. I'm just...I'm so predictably bad at this."

He tipped forward a little, catching her eye. "I think you're probably better at it than you realize. And in case I wasn't clear before, you *are* beautiful, Jordan. Now, then, always."

He gave her such a sweet smile Jordan had to let go of his arm to press a finger under each eye. "I might cry."

"That's okay," Gaines reassured her.

"Yes, but I also might…" She broke off, unable to continue.

He gave her what she had always thought of as his rogue smile, except now she realized he wasn't a rogue, not at all, not even a little. "What else have you got, Jordy? Let me have it."

And so she did, almost lunging across the console in her haste to kiss him. She had no idea if she meant it to be a quick press of lips, mostly because she gave it no forethought, but as soon as her lips touched his all thoughts of quick or simple flew out the window, along with her restraint.

Kissing Gaines was as good as she'd always imagined it would be, if she had allowed herself to imagine such a thing, which she hadn't done until shockingly recently. But it had been a long time since she'd kissed anyone besides Jay, and at that it had been mostly perfunctory hello or goodbye kisses the last few years of parenthood. At first she was on sensory overload. She might have been kissing anyone and overwhelmed by it. And then her brain caught up and she realized she was kissing Gaines. *Gaines.* And he was kissing her back, quite artfully. So much that she sighed against his lips. Her fingers slid into his hair, his fingers caressed her jaw. Jordan had no idea what might have happened next, nor how long they sat in her car kissing like teenagers, but eventually a horn honked, startling them apart.

Abruptly she yanked back, staring at him, mouth ajar with shock, lips bee stung with his kisses.

He regarded her in silence, looking strangely subdued. Or perhaps he was merely being a gentleman after she jumped and mangled him, putting him on pure hormone blast.

"Gaines," she whispered, wishing she could dissolve from the combined power of misery and humiliation. What had she done? And how could she undo it?

"Let's go get the kids," Gaines said and then, not waiting for an answer, got out of the car.

CHAPTER 21

Children could be a handy buffer, when you wanted them to be. Over the last three years Jordan had used them for that purpose often, when she was too tired or too spent to argue with Jay. She would keep the children nearby to spare them both from saying something they shouldn't. It was strange to use the same technique now with Gaines. The children, who had been away from her for two hours, which was two hours longer than they were usually away from her, were happy to comply by clinging to her as much as possible.

Once they were safely tucked in the car Nash fell asleep, but Charlotte was happy to fill the silence with chatter over her new friend McKenna and "Mister Dawwen," who, if her description was to be trusted, was every bit as good with children as Amelia had declared him to be.

Whenever Charlotte seemed to be winding down, Jordan asked her a question to keep her going. And when she ran out of questions, Gaines added a few. That was when her heart really sank, when she realized he was also using the children to fill the awkward silence her kiss had left.

Why, why, why had she been so impetuously stupid as to throw herself at him? Especially on the heels of a nice and heartfelt conversation. *You are a ruiner; you ruin everything good.* Her emotions had been all over the place since Jay's death and couldn't be trusted, but this was something else, something different. Her only hope was to appeal to Gaines's mercy, to remind him she was off kilter and irrational and impetuous right now.

The pervading silence told her Charlotte had fallen asleep. "Gaines," she began but didn't get far.

"Home," he declared, pushing the button for the garage. "We're home. Sit tight, I'll carry the kids."

She watched as he did just that, carrying first Nash and then Charlotte into the house. She waited for him to come back and retrieve her, but of course he didn't. With the discomfort now brewing between them he was probably already digging a tunnel and attempting a jailbreak from the house.

She eased inside and saw him standing in Charlotte's doorway, watching her sleep. When she eased up beside him, he whispered.

"What if there really was a man in her room? What if he hurt her?"

"There might have been a man in her room, but I don't think he hurt her. I probed her ever so gently to make certain she hadn't been disturbed. No matter how many ways I tried, she kept insisting he only stood there, never said a word about touching."

Gaines remained frowning fiercely into the room, plotting vengeance, Jordan was certain. The world he inhabited was different from hers, filled with retribution and swift justice. While she might theoretically say she'd harm anyone who hurt her babies, Gaines would make certain of it.

"Gaines," she whispered, touching her fingertips lightly to his.

He jerked like he'd been branded and spun away. "I'm so thirsty. We should get drinks, the pizza will be here soon."

He walked away from her. Jordan followed, whispering his name. "Gaines, wait, please."

But he didn't. So she jumped on his back, wrapping her arms and legs around him like a needy koala. It wasn't dignified, but it got the job done because he paused, sighing in defeat. "Yes?"

"Please," she pled. "Let me talk."

"I can't," he croaked. They stood in front of the front door. Jordan could see their reflection in the floor to ceiling glass. Gaines looked as pained as they both felt.

"Please," she said, a plaintive whisper close to his ear.

He closed his eyes. "What?"

"I'm so…"

That was as far as she got because he interrupted, spinning abruptly so she was in front of him instead of on his back. He gripped her shoulders, digging his fingers in so it might have been painful if she wasn't in shock. "Please don't apologize, *please,* Jordan. I can take anything but you apologizing for that kiss."

She searched his features, unable to understand his sudden vehemence. In her mind she owed him an apology, so it must be some male issue of pride that demanded her silence. Slowly, tentatively, she rested her palms on his chest, choosing her words carefully. "I'm not sorry about the kiss, Gaines."

Gradually his eyes met hers, some hope restored. "You're not?"

She shook her head and offered up a smile. "That was a great kiss, epic, actually."

"Yeah?" he said, shifting his grip from a clutch to an embrace.

She nodded. "But…"

"Don't say but," he urged, shaking his head slowly.

"However, I am sorry I did that without permission."

He blinked at her. "That's why you're upset? You think I minded?"

She nodded.

He shook his head.

"Oh," she said. Nervously she licked her lips. His eyes followed the trail of her tongue. "I'm very confused."

"I imagine so."

"Jay's only been gone six weeks and he…" she started to say he wouldn't have approved but quickly realized that wasn't true. When they had discussed the very real possibility of his early demise, he had always stated he never wanted her to remain alone and in mourning forever. *I want you to be taken care of, Jordy. Just find someone good who will love you and the kids the way I would have.* No one could possibly do that better than Gaines, his best friend. "What is happening here?"

He took a deep breath, held it, and let it out slowly. When he spoke, his words were measured, careful. "You and I are friends."

She gave a nod of assent.

"We've been friends a long time."

"Thirteen years," she interjected.

"Jay's death hit hard, for both of us."

She nodded, feeling oddly disappointed. This was his way of letting her down easy. Of course. They were discombobulated and grieving, that was all this was. She knew, and yet it hurt somehow to hear him say it.

"And I think," Gaines continued, but now her face was between his hands and he was kissing her eyelids, nose, cheeks and chin. Jordan made a ridiculous little sound, something between a sigh and a whimper, though she was too far gone to care. "I really think," he added before kissing her again, this time on the lips.

Jordan stood on her toes, abandoning herself to the kiss, to *him*. Kissing Gaines was sublime and delicious and every other over-the-top adjective her brain could conjure. At some point she supposed reason might have returned, but they never got to find out because his phone beeped and then beeped again, with an urgency that couldn't be ignored.

Gaines rested his forehead against hers, breathing hard. "It's work."

She gave a little nod, giving her assent. In the game of woman vs. work, she always knew the woman lost. She'd had thirteen years to learn the lesson, after all.

Gaines took his phone from his pocket and flicked it. The harsh light from the little device made Jordan realize how late it had grown. She needed to wake the kids from their late nap or they'd never sleep tonight. But instead she remained frozen as a creeping sort of numbness stole over her. She knew what was coming; she could tell from his expression.

"I have to go," he said, regret and misery mingling with the pending adrenaline of a new assignment. There was never any dread when they had to go away, and maybe that was what hurt the most. The fact that it was so easy for them to leave when it was so hard to remain behind.

"How long?" she asked. Her tone sounded wooden. She didn't want it to. It wasn't the same as with Jay. She had no claim on Gaines; he owed her nothing. But it was a harsh reminder of the last thirteen years, one she was unprepared to feel so soon after that kiss.

"Open ended," he said, meaning he would return after the assignment ended, whenever that might be. A day, a month, a year...who could know?

She looked away, unable to bear whatever her face might reveal in this moment. "Charlotte's birthday..." As soon as the words were out she regretted them. He was doubtless being sent on a matter of national security and importance. Someone somewhere in the world needed him, but so did her little girl. She pressed her lips together and refused to say more.

Gaines's misery increased. "I'll try. I swear I'll try, Jordy. Can you look at me?"

She dragged her eyes back to him and he winced. "I hate leaving like this."

"It's okay. I'm used to it."

That made him wince harder. "If anything happens, anything at all, call the locals. That will alert Ridge. He or Ethan will come, okay?"

She nodded, trying to muster a smile. Navy Wife Rule 101: always send them off with a smile. *I'm so tired of smiling,* she thought, forcing herself to smile harder.

Gaines glanced regretfully toward the kids' rooms. "I don't want to disturb them. Will you kiss them goodbye for me?"

"Absolutely," Jordan said, lips rubbery from all the smiling.

He crushed her in a fierce hug and she returned it, because she didn't have to fake that. She wanted, no, *needed* him to understand that.

"When I come home, we'll talk."

"Yes," she agreed. She closed her eyes and inhaled deeply, storing his scent the way she used to store Jay's. "Hey," she eased back and gave his lapels a little tug. "Take care of you, okay?"

"Take care of you," he returned, leaning forward to kiss her cheek. She was glad for that, glad he seemed to understand she couldn't do more than that right now. He stepped back and, after one more regretful glance, walked out the door.

Jordan made herself wait until his car started and drove away before she dodged to the bathroom and heaved into the toilet.

CHAPTER 22

The first two weeks after Gaines went away were worse than the first six weeks after Jay's death. Jordan couldn't understand why she had powered through the loss of her husband with barely a dent and then came completely undone when Gaines went away. Surely not because she hadn't loved Jay, because she had. They'd been married, had built a life and had children together. As much as she cared about Gaines, their relationship couldn't compare, at least not yet.

The day after he went on assignment, Jordan could barely get out of bed. Only her kids and their need of her kept her moving.

The first day is always the hardest, she told herself, but she knew from past experience it was a lie. The first day was full of momentum. It wasn't until late in the game that things seemed impossible. This time, however, everything hurt. Her mind kept coming back to why. Why did it hurt so much that Gaines went away? Why did it feel like a betrayal? She knew it wasn't. Her mind told her so. Gaines was her friend, an independent person with every right to do his job. She had no claim on him, and neither did the kids. He hadn't abandoned them, was only doing his job. Her reaction was overt and unfair. And yet it was her reaction—pain, betrayal, and grief, so much grief.

She felt like she needed to talk to someone, but she had no idea who that might be. All her friends were military wives whose husbands were still alive. She knew no other widows, and certainly not any in her unique situation. And what situation was that? The one where she'd fallen for a guy so soon after her husband's passing. Try admitting that to a stranger.

The oddity of her situation made her isolation more severe. Absolutely no one could understand. The loneliness, confusion, and grief made Jordan feel like she was collapsing in on herself. And yet she powered on, because of her kids. They'd already lost one parent. They couldn't lose her, too, if only in spirit.

So she kept stumbling forward, day after day, feeling like the walking wounded. At some point she became numb. A part of her brain signaled her that was probably worse somehow, but she couldn't seem to care. Amelia called and texted, as did Maggie. Even Babs tried a time or two, and she was a new friend. Charlotte's party loomed, Jordan did nothing to help it arrive.

Precisely two weeks after Gaines left on assignment, someone knocked on her door. It was a light knock and Jordan steeled herself in case it was her nosy neighbor, come to enquire why she hadn't seen Jordan out and about lately or some other nosy question cloaked in care.

When she opened the door, she didn't recognize the woman on the other side. And yet she was familiar somehow, as if Jordan should know her, if she tried hard enough. Weirder still, she was beaming as she held out a pie, indicating Jordan should take it.

"Why, hello," the woman said, placing the heavy pie in Jordan's hands.

"Hello," Jordan said, sounding as baffled as she felt. "Do I know you?"

"I should think not. We've never met. A shame, wouldn't you say?"

"Yes?" Jordan tried. Her eyes landed on the pie, pecan. "And thank you?"

"You're quite welcome. My name is Juniper. I would shake your hand, but I've recently filled them with pie."

"Oh, right. Let me set this down. Please come in?" She said it like a question again because she wasn't certain she should invite a stranger inside. But she was petite and well-kept, sixty if she was a day.

"Yes, ma'am," Juniper said, closing the door behind her as she stepped inside and followed Jordan to the kitchen. Her eyes skittered everywhere as they progressed. Jordan cringed at the mess, but Juniper smiled. Her finger touched a piece of artwork haplessly taped to the wall. "I remember these days." Her tone was fond and nostalgic.

"You have children?" Jordan inquired.

"Yes, ma'am. Three girls. And now three sons-in-law and a couple of grands." She paused to beam again, clearly delighted.

"Congratulations," Jordan said, returning her smile.

"Thank you."

It was hard not to be charmed by her, between the pie, the dimpling smile, and the overt southern accent. On the other hand, "I'm so sorry, but who are you?"

Juniper snapped to attention. "Oh, dear, did no one tell you I was coming? I thought Cameron might have warned you."

"You know Cam?" Jordan asked.

"We're practically family. His brother is married to my oldest daughter."

Jordan frowned, puzzled. "But I thought Cam's brother was married to The Colonel's daughter."

Juniper's smile turned wry. "Well, I'm not The Colonel, but we do have a fair amount in common. Most notably three children and a predilection for pecans."

"You're his wife," Jordan breathed, awed. The woman was almost as legendary as the man himself. So much that several people doubted her existence, like a Yeti. And yet here she was, alive and well in Jordan's kitchen, and Jordan couldn't fathom why.

"Yes, ma'am," Juniper agreed. "I was so sorry to hear about your husband. We attended his funeral, but kept to the background. John tends to attract a certain amount of notoriety. We didn't want to detract."

"Thank you, that was so kind. I'm sorry I didn't see or speak to you. The day was a bit of a blur."

"Days like those tend to be."

Now it was Jordan's turn to jump to attention as she remembered her manners. "Would you like to sit down? May I get you a drink?" Her hand flapped toward the now-cold coffee she'd forgotten. Juniper's eyes landed there, too, knowingly.

"I would love to sit down, and I don't care for anything to drink, thank you. I can't help but notice the quiet. I hope I'm not taking you away from naptime?" Naptime was gold, as every mother knew.

"Don't give it a thought. It's almost over, anyway." Her eyes darted to the clock before leading Juniper to the couch. She had to move aside a pile of stuffed animals and cracker crumbs before they sat. Juniper seemed not to notice the mess, instead regarding Jordan with a tipped head and inquisitive expression.

"Jordan, our world is small, as I'm certain you know. My husband keeps close tabs on the men under his command, but I take more of an interest in their wives and families. I thought I would stop by and see how you're doing because we have something in common."

"Were you married before The Colonel?"

"No. But shortly before John and I were married I lost my entire family in a car accident. My parents and all my siblings."

"I...I'm so sorry," Jordan stammered, shocked by the ease with which she related her massive and catastrophic loss.

"Thank you. Once you lose someone, you understand. It's an exclusive club absolutely no one wants to join," Juniper said. "And then there's being a military wife. Not so easy, when you get right down to it."

"It's not," Jordan agreed. "Though I guess I'm not one anymore."

"Nonsense," Juniper scoffed. "Once you're in, you're never back out again." She tipped her head, regarding Jordan thoughtfully again. "I don't think our men always understand the toll it takes, do you?"

"It's not the same for them. They get to go away and do something important while we..."

"Stay here and do something important, but perhaps less glamorous," Juniper suggested.

"Yes," Jordan nodded, relieved to have someone who understood the struggle. She had tried so hard not to complain, but she was exhausted.

"Some of our men come back with PTSD, which is a shame and a struggle and I sympathize. But something that gets overlooked, I think, is how many women have to deal with it, too. Both as the support for their struggling husbands and in regard to their own trauma. And it is a trauma, is it not? The constancy of being alone, of moving when you begin to establish new roots, of starting over and being left behind."

Painful tears formed in Jordan's eyes, refusing to be released.

"You've had a lot going on," Juniper said, tone oozing sympathetic understanding, and at last Jordan's dam broke. The tears burst free and made hot, fast tracks down her cheeks. She nodded, unable to speak.

Juniper scooted closer and took her hand, giving it a squeeze. "Here's what I want to tell you. Not that it gets better, because I'm certain you know it does. Eventually, in some way or shape. What I want to say to you is that it's okay if it's not right now. It's okay to wallow, to struggle, to grieve in any way you want or need, for any length of time. Stop pressuring yourself to be okay. Someday you will be. It doesn't have to be now."

Jordan nodded fiercely, doing absolutely nothing to stop her mad rush of tears, mostly because they felt *so good*. She hadn't realized she'd been holding back, that she'd been yearning for permission to cry free, to fall apart, to not be okay. But this woman, this revered, mythical matron was giving her an out, had provided a loophole. Because if The Colonel's wife said it was all right to have a complete and utter breakdown, then it was certainly okay. Maybe even sanctioned.

She sobbed for what felt like hours, heaving, wrenching ugly things that wracked her body and made her throat ache. Juniper sat placidly beside her without touching, as if bearing witness. Somehow that helped, too. Jordan didn't want to be hugged or comforted. She wanted to get it all out, an emotional purge.

Eventually she did. The heaving sobs gave way to shudders and then to sniffles. She felt as though she'd cried for everything that had ever happened to her, not only Jay's death, but all of his accumulated absences, all the things she'd had to face on her own. In a way, she had been a soldier, too. Unpaid and unacknowledged, but expected to carry a heavy burden nonetheless.

"There now," Juniper said cheerfully, as if they'd just finished a craft project together. It made Jordan laugh.

"Juniper, thank you for this. Truly. You've changed my life." Jordan felt she might have gone on for years with this unacknowledged ache, staggering under the weight of her baggage, guilty because the love and care of her family somehow wasn't enough.

"You're welcome. And someday, Jordan, you'll be in a place to help someone else. I promise you."

That was a happy thought for Jordan, she who preferred to care instead of be cared for. In his room, Nash began to cry.

"I believe that's my cue," Juniper said, standing.

"Please stay. Have some pie. The kids would love to meet you."

"And I would love to meet them, but I have a prior commitment."

Just like that she took her leave, gone so quickly it was as if she'd never existed. If not for the pie she'd left in her wake, Jordan might have believed she'd been visited by an angel. Worse, it was too private and tender to gossip over, meaning it would remain a secret. Once again The Colonel's elusive wife would remain a myth and, to Jordan, a legend.

CHAPTER 23

"Why does this entire country smell like falafel?" Logan complained.

"That's your upper lip," Eliza returned, earning a fist bump from Ribs. She was one of those women who was equally good at being a guy, a good thing when she worked with them in such close proximity.

Logan was right too, though. The country did smell. Not like falafel, but putrid and hot, like necrosis and disease. Or maybe it was merely his imagination because it was Not Home and anywhere Not Home at the moment was instinctively bad. When he said he wanted to go home, he didn't picture his waste of space house, the place he somehow never got around to making cozy, the uncomfortable, badly furnished little dwelling. His mind referred instead to Jordan and Nash and Charlotte. At last he'd found something he loved more than his job, and it was his bad luck that his job had been the thing to drive a wedge between them. Both physically and otherwise. His mind kept coming back to the look on Jordan's face when he left her, when she realized she was once again back in that place of relying on a part-time person, someone who could only be there on occasion.

In that instant, in the moment he saw her face, he understood everything Ridge had been trying to tell him—the toll Shimmer's job had taken on her, the toll *his* job would take on her if they continued on this path. It had been a gut punch, all of it, and the clock was still ticking on Charlotte's birthday. Somehow he felt like that was a make-or-break event, that if he could arrive home in time it would restore Jordan's faith in him, her willingness to give them a try.

It was also time to be honest; it wasn't looking good.

"Man, why doesn't he do something?" Logan complained.

Logan and Eliza were young, impetuous, and impatient. It was up to Ribs, the seasoned agent, to keep them in check. But at the moment he agreed with Logan. Boredom was a killer, one they'd had too much of on this assignment. It felt pointless to be here when he could be so much more productive at home.

"Tell me again why we can't flush him out," Eliza demanded.

"Because…" Ribs began, but lacked the will to continue.

"Ah, good point. That's why you're the one in charge," Eliza murmured, staring dully through her scope.

Their target was a Russian suspected of trying to procure a tank for an offshoot of Chechen rebels. Everyone knew he was guilty, but no one wanted to touch him without proof. The Chechens were too desperate for any outside help. The Russians were afraid of his political allies in the Kremlin, and the Americans feared his source was similarly American. And so they waited and watched, waited and watched, hoping he would make a mistake. He would, Ribs knew, because he was good but not perfect.

"What do we know about this guy?" Ribs asked. He'd asked it so often they were tired of hearing it, but they swallowed their complaints and dutifully answered.

"He's a jerk," Logan said, swiping a hand wearily over his face.

"No, he's a *bro*," Eliza clarified.

Logan and Ribs looked at her because this was something new, something she hadn't said before. And that meant she'd been pondering. Eliza's insights, odd as they were, could be invaluable.

"Expand on that," Ribs said, using a nearby pencil to poke her.

She batted the pencil away with an annoyed swipe, absently

rubbing the spot he'd poked. "A jerk is anyone with a bad attitude or grudge. A bro is someone who adds entitlement into that mix. They *can* be charming, until they choose not to be."

Ribs stared thoughtfully at their target, now a blurry image, too many meters away to be in focus.

"Something's happening," Logan said, poking Eliza as he studied Ribs's face.

"Why does everyone keep poking me?" Eliza exploded, giving Logan a hard shove.

"He has the look," Logan hissed.

Now Eliza studied Ribs, smiling when she saw him staring intently. "Good, then maybe we can go home. My weird, old-maid, cat-lady lifestyle isn't going to nurture itself from over here." She fluffed her hair, patting whatever strange hairstyle she'd come up with that day.

"Eliza," Ribs said at last, slowly swiveling his attention to her instead of their far away target. "How would you feel about going Ugly American on us?"

Eliza grinned, preening. "Why, boss, I'd be delighted."

"Yes," Logan exclaimed, already gathering their things and tossing them haphazardly in his bag.

An hour later Eliza reached the front of the line for a latte.

"Excuse me," she said, leaning farther over the counter than propriety allowed. "I asked for an inch of foam. This is barely a skim."

The barista frowned, an easy thing to do because he had the heavy brow of his ancestors. "Is latte. Foam is for cappuccino."

"I wanted a latte *with foam*," Eliza insisted, shoving the cup at him. "Please make it again."

"You want I make cappuccino, I will charge you for cappuccino. Otherwise, enjoy latte," the barista said, his accent becoming almost too thick to discern in his irritation.

"I want what I paid for, which was a latte *with an inch of foam.*" Eliza held the cup aloft, jangling it.

The beleaguered barista, realizing she wouldn't go away, grabbed the cup out of her hand, dumped it, and began making her drink anew. "Thank you," Eliza exclaimed, loudly and full of sarcasm.

The barista muttered a few words in his own language that did not sound like endearments.

Behind her, the customer sighed. Eliza whirled on him. "You got a problem?"

"This isn't Starbucks," he said, his accent clipped and precise. He pointed to the quaint wooden sign over the coffee shop's interior, one that proclaimed it the thirsty trout, if her quick translation was correct. Picturing a trout in relation to coffee made her answering grimace authentic.

"If it were, maybe I'd have a better chance of getting my drink order made right."

"Americans," the customer said, shaking his head. Behind the counter the barista grunted his heartfelt agreement.

"Listen, we saved your life in World War II. Just smile and say thanks." She put out a hand and poked the man in the chest. With that small gesture his demeanor went from annoyed to dangerously icy.

"We were on the same side in World War II, you imbecile, and do not ever touch me."

Eliza let her lower lip quiver dramatically before bursting into noisy, disruptive tears that caused several more people in the café to look at her in disgust. She found it telling that they were more disturbed by her tears than her unruly outburst.

"Is there a problem?" Ribs asked, stepping from the tail end of the line.

"This man insulted me," Eliza exclaimed, pointing at their target. "All I'm trying to do is get a coffee and he…is…so…mean." Here she put both hands over her face and wept, feeling a genuine bitterness over her ruined mascara. Waterproof my Aunt Fanny. And she'd forgotten to pack makeup remover. Her face would be streaked like a comic book character for days after this.

Ribs scowled at the man. "Mister, I don't know where you're from, but where I come from, we don't pick on women."

"This is unbelievable," the man said. "You Americans are deranged. This woman is being obnoxiously abusive to the wait staff and you're taking her side because of a few tears."

Ribs made a show of inspecting Eliza who dabbed at her eyes and shuddered pathetically. Naturally small, she looked tiny and harmless next to the two larger men. "This woman?" Ribs asked, incredulous as he pointed to Eliza.

"She...the..." The target spluttered, pointing between Eliza and the counter. At another time it would have been a delicious victory because the man wasn't the sort to splutter. But they needed more from him, so much more.

Ribs took a tiny step forward, straightening. "I don't like your tone. Maybe someone needs to teach you a lesson about picking on someone your own size."

The target straightened, losing the bluster. "Trust me when I tell you that you do not want a piece of me, as your saying goes. It would go better for you if you turn and walk away right now, taking the idiot American millennial with you."

"How about we step outside and settle this like men?" Ribs suggested.

The target sighed and looked away, willfully ignoring him.

Ribs placed a hand on his chest and gave him a provoking shove.

The target showed no reaction.

Eliza placed a hand on Ribs's arm. "It's nice what you're trying to do, but I'm afraid it's wasted effort. Obviously this German cretin has no concept of American chivalry. And for the record, I am not a millennial; I'm Gen Z, Grandpa."

His eyes snapped back to Eliza, explosive with fire. "I am not German," he ground out.

She had to make herself refrain from glancing at Ribs, but really? Everything they'd thrown at him, and that was what stuck? "Could have fooled me, Adolf," she said softly, sickly sweet. She reached over the counter for her drink and he lunged at her. Only Ribs's quick action kept the man from punching her.

"Out," the barista shouted. "Out of our shop, we want no trouble."

Hand tangled in the back of his shirt, Ribs dragged the man outside, letting him go in time for the man to take a hard swing at him, one big enough to catch the attention of the police officer who'd been tipped off about an illegally parked car. Hastily, he stuffed his ticket book away and reached for his nightstick, brandishing it at the target.

"What is going on?" he roared, or at least that was what Eliza presumed he said in his language. It had that tone, however.

Ribs backed down and tried to look innocent, something he was able to accomplish after so many years of being a good actor. And now it was only the target that was enraged and blustering, a stuck bull.

He tried to tell the cop about Eliza's bad behavior in the shop, Ribs's ill-placed machismo, but he was the one yelling like a madman and waving his hands while Ribs and Eliza stood innocently by. Eliza sniffled between sips of her coffee. The officer kept darting her glances, which was unfortunate timing because he was *cute*. She could appreciate that, even when she was on duty. But there was no time for exploration, only confuscation and escalation, something that happened naturally now that the officer was involved and seemed to be taking their side.

"Have you gone mad?" their target demanded. "These two…" he motioned toward Eliza and Ribs, unable to think of an adjective dire enough to describe them. "*Americans*," he hissed at last, tone stuffed with loathing, "are everything wrong with the world right now, and you are trying to make me the problem."

"My tourist agency assured me this area was safe," Eliza said, words wobbly to match her leaky eyes. "They bring people here all the time. What are they going to say when I tell them I've been manhandled?"

That did it. Tourism was up and coming in this part of the world, highly sought after for the money it would bring. If there was one thing everyone in the city agreed on, it was the need to keep the tourists happy.

"I think we should discuss this downtown," the officer said. He was young and eager to impress, in this case it worked well for them that the person he seemed most eager to impress was Eliza. She gave an encouraging nod and he pulled out his cuffs.

The target exploded, now prepared to take a swing at the cop, but Ribs dropped the innocent act and gave him a look. Puzzled now, the man stared inquiringly at Ribs as the officer cuffed him behind his back.

"We'll merely have a conversation in a less public environment," the officer assured him, but the wheels of bureaucracy were such that it would take hours before he was released, a fact Ribs and his team counted on.

The man stared at Ribs afresh, with dawning horror that this was something more than a mere annoyance. The officer tucked him into the back of the car, and Ribs gave him a little salute, pressing his finger to his ear when Logan spoke.

"I'm in. Oh, man, this guy is not good at hiding his tracks."

Ribs put his arm companionably on Eliza's shoulders and herded her toward the target's apartment. "Kudos on being as obnoxious as humanly possible, Eliza."

"Thank you. I learned it from my mom," Eliza said, ducking her head with false modesty.

Ribs laughed and dropped his arm, suppressing a yawn. "Let's hope our guy is so relentlessly stupid we can tie this up tonight and go home."

"Are you sure I shouldn't go to the station, oversee things?" She stared hopefully after the target, along with the cute cop who'd taken him.

"There are plenty of boys back home," Ribs assured her.

"None I've found," she said with a sigh, facing forward again.

"Sometimes it takes a while," he comforted. Thirteen years, in fact.

"You're a good dad," Eliza said, linking arms with him.

"I hope to be," Ribs returned.

"Oh, geez, you've gone all earnest. Stop it, you're creeping me out." She dropped his arm and gave it a shove.

"Does it help that I'm about to break into someone's house and rifle their most treasured possessions?" he asked.

She pressed a finger to her cheek, thinking. "It does, a little. Thanks."

"Anytime," he said, holding out his fist for a bump. She returned it, and they walked in companionable silence to the target's house.

CHAPTER 24

"Should a child's birthday party bring me this close to the brink of sanity?" Jordan wondered out loud.

"There's been kind of a lot going on," Maggie assured her, removing a tray of cookies from the oven.

"Yes, but I'm pretty sure it would always be this way, regardless of anything else," Jordan said, blowing her fingers before using them to transfer the hot cookies. She had a spatula…somewhere. "Some people take to motherhood more naturally."

"Stop being so hard on yourself. Everyone's a mess in our own special way," Maggie chastised, putting another tray into the oven.

"Some people just look better doing it," Amelia agreed, smoothing her flawless tresses. She was the one cutting the cookies and putting them on a tray. "These cookies, for example, aren't perfect. They're a little lumpy and misshapen, but slather some good tasting frosting on top and no one will care."

The two sisters paused and looked at each other. "Except Darren," they said together.

"Five bucks says he comments on it before he takes a bite," Amelia said.

"I'm not taking that bet," Maggie countered.

"He's so great with the kids," Jordan added helpfully. She had yet to see the side of Darren his sisters saw, the critical perfectionist who struggled to keep his opinions to himself. All she had witnessed so far was the nice guy who adored his wife and stepdaughter.

"He is that," Amelia grudgingly agreed.

"And he's trying to do better. He'll comment on the cookie, but he'll laugh and eat it anyway," Maggie said loyally.

"And then probably comment on how good they taste, despite the imperfection," Amelia agreed. "I forgot what we were originally talking about."

"Feeling overwhelmed," Maggie reminded her.

"Ah," Amelia said. "But that's why we're here, to help manage the whelm."

"And you do," Jordan told them, feeling a rush of warmth for their bolstering presence. It wasn't everyone who would give up an afternoon to help prep for a four year old's birthday party.

"You had us at cookies," Maggie said, stuffing one in her mouth while Jordan and Amelia looked on. "What? It was broken."

"I saw you break it," Amelia accused.

"So?" Maggie said.

"So you didn't give me any," Amelia returned, holding out her hand.

Dutifully, Maggie gave her a cookie. Amelia chewed and swallowed before she spoke again. "Is Ribs going to make it?"

Jordan's heart did the swoop and dive thing it had been doing whenever anyone mentioned Gaines lately. "I haven't heard a word since he went away."

Amelia huffed in disgust. "Stupid spy stuff."

"It pays the bills," Ethan said. He had let himself in and now joined them in the kitchen. "What can I do?"

"Nothing now, but you can man the grill when the time comes," Jordan told him.

"Yes," he hissed, pumping his fist.

"Any sign of my husband?" Maggie asked. Ridge always stayed later than everybody else.

"I think he's making an early exit today, another hour, tops," Ethan told her.

"I told the kids I'd steal them a snack," Darren said, poking his head in the kitchen.

"Babs is on her way," Ethan assured him.

"I know, she texted." Darren's eyes landed on the cookies Amelia was putting on a tray. "You're not chilling that? It's going to come out misshape…Oh." His eyes landed on the zaftig ones that were already baked. He shrugged and picked one up. "Tastes good, though," he added, covering his mouth as he chewed.

Amelia and Maggie exchanged a surreptitious glance. Jordan smiled, feeling cheered and filled up at the benevolent scene. Everyone was here because they cared about her and her family, in a tangible way. And since her talk with Juniper she could fully engage in the moment and appreciate that fact. Her world was far from perfect, but this moment was as close as she could possibly get. The only thing that would make it better would be… But no, she wouldn't put that on him. Gaines had a job to do, and he would be there if he could. If not…

No, she wouldn't think about it now. She would enjoy this moment, so filled with love, and be happy.

Babs arrived, followed by Ridge. Ethan manned the grill while the men offered unsolicited tips on how to do it better. Charlotte, Nash, and McKenna ran or crawled through everyone's legs, Maggie and Ridge's baby was alternately passed around and loved on while the women arranged the remainder of the food.

Jordan stood back, observing, a strange mix of happiness and sadness, love and yearning. So many days had been spent like this, but with Jay present. He would have manned the grill possessively, dismissing the unasked for advice with disdain. Only Gaines had been allowed to grill in his absence, and there could probably be a metaphor in there, if she was inclined to search for it. The void he left felt painful and empty, but not as much as she feared. Sort of like poking a bruise. If you didn't know it was there, you might forget about it, but as soon as you touched it the reminder made it hurt. She guessed there would be a lot of days like this one, where unexpected reminders rehashed pain she thought she'd already resolved. At the same time she felt good and whole and loved, and that was what Jordan chose to take away from the day, that she could feel more than one thing at any given moment. Life wasn't all good or all bad, all happy or all sad. Instead it was a complex mix of everything. Her attitude and choice to dwell on the more positive aspects would determine her future, as well as that of her children. She could choose to wallow in her grief or embrace the joy in every celebration. Today was a day for celebration. Later she would look through the pictures of Charlotte's birth, pictures of her and Jay and their overwhelming terror/happiness at becoming new parents. Then she would shed tears and feel grief. Right now, in this moment, there was only tenderness and light.

She had told everyone no presents, but of course everyone ignored her. Charlotte was in a frenzy of delight at the attention, making Jordan happy to be overridden. Her daughter squealed as she opened each present, then hopped off Jordan's lap and went to hug the giver.

Finally Ethan handed Jordan an oversized package with a chagrined smile. "He said to give it to you if he didn't make it in time. I hope that's okay."

Whether it was okay or not was a moot point when Charlotte grabbed it and tore it open, revealing another oversized stuffed dog.

"It wooks wike you," Charlotte said, holding the dog aloft with unaccustomed restraint. Usually by now she'd be squealing and hugging it, but instead she held it out for Jordan's inspection. And Jordan could see that in some strange way, the dog indeed resembled her, with startlingly blue eyes and a tuft of blond hair on top.

"They match," Ethan, ever the pot stirrer, said as he lined up the new dog by Wibs, who looked a little worse for wear after being loved on so much the last few weeks. "Might need to sharpie a giant scar on this one." His finger trailed down Wibs's ribcage.

"Oh, my lands, Ethan, you're making me blush," Jordan said, giving his shoulder a shove.

"What?" Ethan asked with feigned innocence. "All I'm saying is that they match and go together in an eternal sort of way."

"They're getting married," Charlotte announced, so decidedly deadpan everyone fell silent and turned to look at her. Then she held up her two dogs, side by side, and made them kiss.

"Maybe…" Ethan began, but this time Amelia put a hand over his mouth, halting whatever he was going to say next.

"Stop it. If Jordan blushes any harder she's going to bust a capillary and throw off the highlights I laboriously put into her hair."

Later, when the kids were occupied with Charlotte's new toys, Ridge eased closer. "Anything else weird happen lately?"

"I spent more than a decade married to a SEAL turned spy. Define weird," Jordan said, and he laughed.

"Noises, sightings, that sort of thing."

"Ah. No, not a thing. Everything has been so normal I'm gaslighting myself. Maybe it was all in my mind? I was pretty over-whelmed and exhausted there for a while. I suppose it's possible I imagined noises and people where there were none." She frowned, not liking that scenario. Even giving herself an out because of the emotional duress didn't sit right. Jordan had never been the type of person to become hysterical or suffer a drama-fueled imagination.

"Maybe," Ridge agreed, but he looked disturbed, too. "Just remember to charge your phone every night and keep it by the bed."

"Okay," she agreed, smiling. Jay had once told her that Ridge couldn't stop himself from being the big brother of the group, even if he tried.

"Also…" His finger dipped around the edge of his glass and he avoided eye contact, two signs he was about to delve into the uncomfortable personal realm. "He's trying, okay? He's really trying to figure it out. Family stuff is new for him."

"I know," Jordan agreed. "And I appreciate that. The problem isn't him, though. It's me. Because he might be new to the family stuff, but I've lived with the military and spy stuff a long time and, no offense to you or Maggie, but I just don't think I can do it. Ever again." The finality of her words threatened to upend the happiness she'd vowed to claim today, but she couldn't see a way out of the tunnel. After her talk with Juniper she realized how much trauma she'd been holding onto, trauma inflicted on her by the United States Government. For her sanity, for the sake of her children, she couldn't go back to that life again, now that she'd been handed a reprieve.

Ridge gave a little nod of understanding but didn't offer further advice. Maggie and Amelia came to claim her to help the kids decorate their cookies, and she was able to reclaim the fun she had started to lose. They stayed to help clean up, so after everyone was gone all she had to do was tuck the kids into bed, and she was free to...what?

She had no idea, and nothing came to mind as she wandered restlessly from room to room, searching for something to fill her mind. Her shelf was stacked with half read books she'd grown too sleepy to finish. Her closet had a couple of knitting projects she started before the kids were born and never picked up again. The television held promise, but when she sat and turned it on, nothing snagged her attention. Eventually she stared listlessly into space until she realized the furry thing beside her foot was Charlotte's stuffed dog. She must have been really zonked if she went to bed without it because she never went to bed without it.

Jordan picked it up, realizing as she did so that both dogs were there. She held them both aloft, staring at them side by side.

"You guys look good together," she whispered. "Like you belong."

They didn't answer back, obviously, so she tucked one under each arm, intending to deposit them in Charlotte's room. But a few minutes later, she was asleep.

CHAPTER 25

She was having the dream again. Only this time Jay wasn't in it. The person beside her, the person pressing his lips on hers was all Gaines. Except it wasn't because the smell was off. Even in her dream she recognized that fact. And the feel of his lips, she knew now from experience, wasn't the same.

Her eyes popped open. A man hovered over her face, his fetid breath blowing into her mouth, the mouth he'd just kissed. Jordan yelped. The man scrambled away and fell backwards over the coffee table.

Her phone, where was her phone? *Ridge told me to keep it beside my bed.* That was what she had done, as soon as everyone left, never guessing she would fall asleep in the living room. She darted off the couch and toward her room, only later realizing her mistake. She was a sitting duck there, easy to round up and contain, except that the man didn't pursue her.

She grabbed her phone and, with shaking fingers, dialed 911. The dispatcher remained on the line with her while she checked the kids' rooms. As before their doors were open, when she was certain she'd closed them. But the children were undisturbed and unaware of her terror, lucky them. Jordan wasn't certain she would ever sleep again after this night.

"The kids are okay," she told the dispatcher. "They're still sleeping." She leaned against the wall outside Charlotte's room, eyes closed a second before remembering she needed to keep them open. The man, so able to appear and disappear, could show up in a blink. And he did.

As soon as she opened her eyes she saw him standing in front of her.

"It's me," Gaines assured her, and she dropped the phone.

"The real you, or am I having the dream again?" she asked.

"You've dreamed about me?" he asked, brows arching.

"Have you dreamed about me?" she countered.

"Ten thousand and one times," he said sincerely.

They realized the dispatcher was trying to get their attention on the phone, now on the floor between them. He reached for it at the same time she did, narrowly avoiding knocking heads. His hands were steady and warm against her shaking ones as he put the phone back in her fingers.

"Talk to the dispatcher, she's frantic," he insisted.

"So am I," she said, voice unsteady. But she followed his command, tucking the phone against her ear. "I'm here, sorry. I dropped the phone. My friend showed up. I'm okay." Gaines reached for her, pulling her against him as he secured her in his warm and solid embrace. "I'm okay," she repeated, this time for his benefit. Her free arm snaked around his waist, latching on. She had missed him *so much.*

"What happened?" he asked. His hand slid beneath her hair, thumb smoothing along her neck.

"I..." she began, but the police arrived. She recounted the story for all of them, the two officers and Gaines.

"Dude kissed you?" one of the officers blurted.

"Yes," she said, scrubbing her hand over her lips with a grimace. It would take something potent to erase the memory of his stale breath and too-thin lips. She glanced at Gaines who stared back at her in horror and concern, protectiveness and anger oozing from his pores.

"We'll take a look around," one of the officers said, swiping a hand over the back of his neck.

"They don't believe me," Jordan said when they'd gone.

"I think they do, but they don't like complex problems with no easy solutions. Neither do I, come to think of it. Hold on, Ridge is burning up my phone. Let me tell him what's up so he won't call in the hounds." He stepped into the kitchen to make the call and even that felt too far away at the moment. Jordan sank to the couch, trying not to shake. She had never been more afraid. The rush of fear, followed by so much adrenaline, had left her weak and spent.

Gaines returned and tossed his phone onto the table before bundling her into his embrace, balled up like a little caterpillar. His face pressed to her neck, inhaling. "I missed you."

"Same," Jordan agreed, suddenly renewed. She had no idea until then that it was possible to receive an energy infusion from another person, but apparently so because her earlier bout of weakness had been replaced by a second shot of adrenaline. This one zapped through her, making her fingers tingle with the need to touch him, to reassure herself he was here. Something was off about him, and she realized what it was; Gaines was rumpled, and Gaines was never rumpled.

"When's the last time you slept?" she murmured.

"Hard to calculate with the time difference." He squinted. "Three days ago, maybe. It took twenty-four hours to get home. I didn't sleep any of it because…"

"Because why?" she asked, pulling away to inspect his face. His cheeks were past stubble and well into beard territory, his eyes red rimmed.

"I had a lot on my mind, and I was trying so hard to get here in time. I'm sorry I missed the party."

"It's okay," she said.

"It's not," he insisted. "And I swear to you it will never happen again."

She gave him a sad smile because she knew better. He might have the best intentions in the world, but those didn't matter when the job came calling. Jay had been there for Charlotte's birth, but he'd missed every birthday since. And all of Jordan's birthdays the last five years, along with their anniversary.

"Jordy," he began, but they were interrupted by the reappearance of the police officer who sighed, exasperated.

"We didn't find anything. We'll keep a patrol. Are you staying?"

"I'm staying," Gaines replied. "We're going to get this figured out." Jordan didn't know if he was talking to her or the officer, but the officers nodded, satisfied, and took their leave.

"I can't help but feel like I'm on a list somewhere, like someone who writes bad checks. If I go to the police station, am I going to see my name somewhere with the words, 'Do Not Believe?'"

"No, but it doesn't matter because I believe you, and I'm not going anywhere. And what I said was true. We are going to get this figured out."

"What do you have in mind, super sleuth?" she asked.

"A secret weapon. Spy stuff." He wagged his brows.

Her sad little heart turned over a few times at that wag. He was so ridiculously appealing, even after three days of no sleep and, presumably, no shower. And yet he still smelled better than the stranger who'd kissed her. "When do I get to find out what it is?" she asked.

He eased closer, brushing his nose on hers. "Right about now, I think."

She thought he was going to kiss her, so it came as something of a disappointing surprise when he stood and headed for the door. In fact it was such a surprise that Jordan tumbled off the couch. When Gaines paused to glance back, she pretended to be picking up a toy from the ground. "Found it," she called, holding the Barbie aloft.

"Smooth," he said, completely on to her. He held out a hand and led her to the door before whoever was there could knock.

A man stood on the other side, hand upraised in a fist. "Spooky, Ribs," he said. "Are you psychic now?"

"No, but you might want to have your muffler checked. Good sneaking, Leo." The men bumped fists, and that was when Jordan noticed the woman. She stood beside Leo, small and nondescript, minus a mane of long, wild curls. Her hair was untamed, but she wore a long homespun dress that was clearly hand-sewn, and in her hands she held a loaf of bread toward Jordan.

"Thank you," Jordan said. As with Juniper it came out like a question. What was it with the women of the world dropping by to bring her baked goods lately? Not that she was complaining. The smell of the bread told her it was going to be good.

"Jordy, this is Leo, I think you've heard us mention. He's on Ridge's team. And this is Esther."

"My wife," Leo added as Esther walked past them and began to look around.

"It's nice to meet you," Jordan said. "Feel free to do whatever it is you need to do." This she addressed to Leo who gave a little chuckle.

"She thinks I'm the one who's here to work."

"You're not?" Jordan asked.

"I drive and carry a gun. This is Esther's gig." He motioned toward his wife who was making her way intently through Jordan's house without a word, laser focused on the walls and windows for some reason.

"Oh," Jordan drawled, not sure what to think. "It's messy, and...we had a party and..." Esther crouched, staring at the baseboard.

"It's fine, she doesn't care. She'll talk to you in a minute. Is it okay if we sit?" Leo asked, already heading toward the couch.

"I...yes?" This time Jordan directed her attention to Gaines who was watching her with rapt attention, as if afraid to take his eyes off her.

Leo sank into the chair with a sigh. "Just got back?" he asked Gaines.

"Came here from the airport," Gaines said, smothering a yawn.

"Man, that's rough," Leo sympathized.

Jordan wanted to watch Esther, but she had disappeared somewhere. "I have two kids," she warned.

"They won't hear her. She's naturally silent," Leo said, unconcerned.

"I don't know if I understand what's happening," Jordan said.

"It's hard to explain," Gaines said, smothering another yawn. He looked so miserably tired. Jordan pulled his head to rest on her shoulder, kissing the top of it. He nestled, and then he was out, leaving her to stare awkwardly at Leo who gave her a reassuring smile in return.

"Esther is uniquely talented at finding hidden clues," Leo explained.

"Better than Gaines?" she asked, somewhat defensively. If Gaines hadn't been able to find anything, she doubted this Esther person could.

"Better than anybody. Her mind puts things together in unthinkable ways. You'll see," he promised.

They sat in silence for a while that was strangely comfortable, given the fact that they were strangers, Gaines slept on her shoulder, and a woman was somewhere nearby roaming her house, looking who knew where for who knew what.

Eventually Esther wandered back into the room, wraithlike. Out of places to sit, she perched on her husband's lap, nestling slightly when he gave her a squeeze. This time she bestowed her attention on Jordan, along with a tiny smile. "Hi, I'm Esther. I'm sorry if I ignored you before. Did I?" She addressed Leo.

"A little. It's fine. Tell us what you found."

"It's like this," Esther began, crossing her hands in her lap.

"Hold on, Ribs," Leo reached out and poked Gaines with his foot. Gaines did the thing where he came immediately awake and alert, as if he'd never been asleep. He clasped Jordan's hand and they all waited for Esther's pronouncement.

"A few years ago my dad fenced in our garden because we were having a problem with rabbits. He dug the fence a couple of feet deep, but the rabbits kept getting in. No matter what he did, the rabbits kept getting in. And then we realized the truth; the rabbits were there all along. We'd fenced them in," Esther said.

It was too much for Jordan to sort, especially so late at night, but Gaines seemed to understand. He stared at Esther in open-mouthed surprise. "You're saying…"

She nodded and pointed over their heads. "The reason there's no sign of entry or exit is because he hasn't come or gone. Your intruder's in the attic."

CHAPTER 26

"Someone is in my attic?" Jordan whispered.

"Right now? He's still there?" Gaines clarified.

"Yes. And based on the evidence I'd say he's been living there about the past couple of months," Esther added. She sounded so deadpan, but that was probably because no one was living in *her* attic, Jordan thought, shuddering.

"I guess this is where I come in," Leo said, moving Esther aside to check his gun. His eyes flicked to Gaines. "You coming?"

"I wouldn't miss it," Gaines replied.

"You're just going to…go get him?" Jordan asked weakly.

"Obviously," Gaines replied. Then, sensing how rattled and upset she was, paused to kiss her cheek and whisper in her ear. "It's going to be okay, Jordy. Back in a minute."

"You'll need to move the little girl. The access point is in her closet," Esther said.

This time Jordan wasn't the only one disturbed. "He's been using Charlotte's room this whole time?" Gaines clarified, knuckles popping.

Esther nodded. "Do you need me to help move her, hold her… something?" She trailed off, sounding uncertain for the first time.

"I'll put her in my bed. She's so exhausted she probably won't even notice," Jordan said. She followed the men to Charlotte's room, shuddering as they stood sentinel by the closet. As she'd predicted, Charlotte was too far gone to stir, even when Jordan deposited her in her oversized bed and slid the covers up.

There was some ruckus overhead as she returned to Esther, though not as much as she might have imagined, and then they were back, leading a dusty looking boy between them, his arm wrenched painfully to the middle of his back as they frog marched him.

"Do you know him?" Gaines asked her.

Jordan made herself look at the boy, or rather young man. If she had to guess, she'd peg him at twenty. He looked familiar somehow, but she was sure she'd never met him. "Were you at Jay's funeral?"

He didn't answer until Gaines twisted his arm, and then he gave a curt nod, avoiding eye contact.

"Who are you?" she asked.

But the boy wouldn't answer, no matter how much Gaines nudged him.

"I think I know," the ever-prescient Esther inserted. Everyone looked at her. She pointed toward the window, out the door, toward the neighbor's house.

"You belong to Nan and Kurt?" Jordan said, but she looked toward Esther for the answer instead of the boy.

"I cross referenced missing people, drifters, registered pedophiles, and domestic complaints on my way here," Esther explained. "There were two calls from your neighbor regarding their son in recent months. One to report erratic behavior and request a psychiatric evaluation, and one to report him missing."

"What are we doing with this guy?" Leo asked.

"I think we need to start with his parents," Jordan said.

"And obviously the police," Gaines added.

The boy jerked like they'd shocked him. "No. Can't you just let me go? Look, I'm sorry. I was trying to do the right thing."

"How so?" Leo asked because Gaines was a little too overheated to respond in a reasonable manner and Jordan was still speechless with shock.

"My parents dragged me to the funeral and I…I don't know. You were all alone and you had these kids. It seemed like someone needed to watch out for you."

"And you thought that should be you," Gaines said, tone derisive. "What about me?"

"You're never here," the boy flung back at him, and it was oddly reminiscent of the fights Jordan had had with Jay the last few months before his death.

She tilted her head at the boy in renewed suspicion. "What's your name?"

"Thomas," he said, tone miserable.

"Thomas, I think you're lying. And I think you've been coming and going from my attic long before my husband died, am I right?" Little noises she'd heard on the nights Jay was away began to make sense.

Thomas shrugged, his expression shifting from plaintive to mutinous, erasing any of Jordan's sympathy. Clearly the boy was troubled. Clearly he needed more help than she or his parents could give. "I think the parents and police are still our best option here," she said.

Gaines tightened his grip on the boy's shoulder. "And you should know that I plan to be here fulltime from now on. Don't come back. I'll be watching."

The boy's answering smirk held a challenge, but so did Gaines's set features. In a contest between the two, Jordan wasn't worried about who would come out on top, and woe to the boy if Gaines ever caught him near her again.

They waited in awkward silence while Leo went to retrieve Nan and Kurt who arrived with tears and anger, tears for Nan, anger for Kurt.

"Of all the…" he began, then apparently ran out of words as he stared at his son. "Tormenting a widow with children. When I heard she was hearing sounds, I wondered, but I never thought you would stoop so low," he finished at last, shaking his head.

"He didn't mean it," Nan volunteered.

"You don't know what he meant," Kurt snapped.

And then the awkward silence descended again until the police arrived. There were interviews, forms to fill, pictures to be snapped until at last the house cleared out. Only Jordan and Gaines, Leo and Esther remained.

"Thank you," Jordan said, feeling drained in light of the night's events and resolution.

"You're welcome," Esther replied, sounding oddly chipper for four in the morning.

"This is her normal wakeup time," Leo explained to Jordan, darting his wife an affectionate glance.

"I was raised on a farm. Old habits die hard," Esther explained.

"Maybe we could have coffee sometime," Jordan inserted before Esther could get away. She was a little different, but likeable and ridiculously interesting. And Gaines clearly liked Leo. Maybe the four of them could…but no, she and Gaines weren't a twosome. She kept forgetting.

Esther gave her the tiny smile again. "I'd really like that."

Behind them Nash began to stir. Jordan pressed a thumb to her forehead, feeling exhausted. "He's never going to wean," she murmured.

"My mom's a midwife. I can tell you exactly how to get a baby to wean," Esther said.

Jordan's brows rose hopefully. "Really? How? Because I've tried everything and I'm getting kind of desperate."

"All you have to do is get pregnant again. Milk turns salty in the second trimester. Babies don't like it and wean themselves."

Leo snorted a laugh and turned it into a cough.

"Was that bad?" Esther asked him, but he merely shook his head. Gaines answered in his stead.

"No that was amazing. Best plan ever." He tossed Jordan a smile, smiling harder when her face turned four shades of purple.

Esther scratched her temple and regarded Leo. "Despite your reassurance, I feel like I said the wrong thing there."

"It was perfect, I promise," Gaines said, ushering them to the door. He waved, closed the door, and leaned against it.

"So that *is* your wolfish smile. I thought so," Jordan said.

"Can't help it if you're all kinds of hot," Gaines said. He left the door and began stalking toward her.

"You must be delirious from lack of sleep. It's the middle of the night and I slept in my makeup and I need a shower and…"

"What did I tell you about believing me when I tell you things?" he warned, continuing his advance.

She took a step back and landed against the back of a chair, feeling suddenly like cornered prey. Her hand came up, attempting to halt him. "Gaines we need to talk."

"I'll say," he agreed, taking her hand and using it to pull her against him.

"I can't be with you," she breathed.

"Why not?" he asked, nibbling her neck.

"Because of your job," she said, standing on her toes to get closer.

"Okay," he said. His thumb caressed her bottom lip and then he kissed it. Jordan so badly wanted to respond, but she was hanging on to reason by a thread and pulled away.

"You're not listening to me, but you have to because I can't do it anymore. I can't do it again. I can't go back to that life of not knowing, of saying goodbye and wondering if I'll ever see you again. I can't do it to me, and especially not to the kids."

"Okay," he agreed.

She huffed a little sigh and stamped her foot. He made the mistake of smiling, but she was so ridiculously cute. "Gaines, would you listen to me and what I'm trying to tell you?"

"Jordan, would you listen to me and what I'm trying to tell you?" he echoed. She attempted to wriggle away. He grasped the front of her pants and hauled her back. "Woman, if you'd stop trying to escape and let me talk I'd tell you that I quit my job."

"You did what?"

He squinted. "You sound mad. That's kind of the opposite of the happy I thought you'd be."

"You quit your job?" she said, slowly and loudly.

He nodded.

"For me?" She pointed to her chest, in case there was any confusion.

"Who else?" he countered.

She looked away, panic stricken, ready to flee again. He captured her hands, holding her in place. "Tell me what's going on here, so I can talk you down."

"I knew you were having some feelings for me, some attraction, but enough to quit your job? Gaines, your job is everything to you. You love your job."

"I like my job, but it's just a job, Jordan. A job can't love you back. What, no, *who* I love is you."

She was still doing the panicked rapid blinky thing. "You don't believe me," he surmised.

"I have my doubts," she said. "We've been friends for so long, and the last few weeks have been intense. I'd rather you take some time and think…" she had to stop talking because he pulled out his phone and began flicking through his contacts. "What are you doing?"

"I'm about to prove a point. This is going to be epic. Before I make this call, answer one question for me: what is my favorite food?"

"Meatloaf," she answered without hesitation.

"Perfect. Hang on." He pushed a button. After a few rings a woman's groggy voice answered.

"There'd better be a stupendous reason you're calling me."

"Hi, Mom. Did I wake you?" He winked at Jordan.

"You know you did not. I just got off work at the hospital and am catching up on *Wheel of Fortune* on my DVR. So I repeat that there better be a good reason to interrupt Pat and Vanna."

"There is. I have an important question."

"I wait with baited breath, child of mine."

"What's my least favorite food, the thing I hate the most in the world?"

She sighed. "Meatloaf. If I had even a portion of the time that I spent trying to get you to eat your meatloaf, I'd be able to finish this show. Why do you ask at five in the morning?"

"Settling a bet with a friend. Give my love to Pat and Vanna."

"Give my love to whichever random and secret thing you're up to." She disconnected without saying goodbye.

"I know I haven't met her, but I love her," Jordan said. "Also, I'm really confused. Gaines, you love meatloaf. You've always loved meatloaf. It's what you asked for the first time you came into my restaurant."

He stuffed his phone away and licked his lips, looking suddenly nervous. "Okay, rewind thirteen years. I'm walking down the street, looking in windows at myself in my nicely fitting uniform, when what do I see but this adorable blond waitress standing behind a counter? I walk in, realize I'm breathless and insensible and say the only thing I can think of."

"'What do you recommend,'" she said with sudden remembrance.

He nodded. "You recommended the meatloaf. I lacked the heart to tell you how much I hated it. So I ordered it and ate every bite."

"But you *always* ordered the meatloaf," she said.

"Because I was desperate to do anything to impress you, to keep you talking, to steal you away and keep you forever."

"Gaines," she exploded, tossing her hands wide. "I have been making you meatloaf on the regular all this time, for *thirteen years*, and I'm just now finding out you loathe it? Why?"

"Because all that time I spent hating meatloaf, I was loving you. I tried so hard and for so long to *not* love you. I guess eating your meatloaf was my one concession to that secret, a tangible way to let myself remember and bask in those feelings."

A little puff of air escaped, but nothing else.

"Say something," he prodded, poking her.

"You don't mean that," she whispered.

He nodded.

"I need a better explanation. Say more words," she said, eyes going teary.

"From that first moment, the first sight of you through that window, I lost my heart. Just totally and completely head over heals gone. But then you met Jay and *you* were gone. So I kind of gave up on the idea of us. But I figured as long as you still held my heart, it would be safe. And so I never really tried to get it back again. I figured I'd go on loving you forever, and you'd never find out. Maybe someday I would find someone I loved as much. But then…"

"But then…" she agreed. A bulldozer could have driven through her house, and she wouldn't have been able to tear her eyes away from Gaines, so vulnerable as he stood before her and made his confession. Suddenly everything in her life reoriented itself and she saw it, saw the way he'd stood on the periphery and loved her from afar. All the times he'd encouraged her, cheered her, helped her, supported her, stood by her, cared for her. Even watched over Jay for her when they were apart.

"You love me. You really love me," she said softly, wonderingly.

"So much, you have no idea." He smoothed his thumbs over the backs of her hands, still held gently in his. "I know it's only been a few weeks since Jay died, Jordy. I know you're not where I am, but I swear I'll love you enough for both of us, if you'll only give me a chance. I promise to…" He stopped talking. He had to, because her lips settled on his, making it impossible.

Nash began to stir again. They rested their foreheads together, trying to catch a breath. "Back to the job thing," she prompted. "Did you really quit?"

"I really did. Effective as of this last assignment."

"What are you going to do instead?"

"I'm going to open my own security firm. I have no idea if it will make it, but I think so. My finances are going to be tight for a while," he warned.

"This is quite the coincidence because I'm looking to hire private security," she said.

"Yeah?" he asked.

She nodded. "Apparently my neighbor kid's been stalking me."

"That sounds like a fulltime problem that's going to require a fulltime solution."

She sucked a breath. "Yikes, sounds expensive. I'm not sure how much I can afford to pay, seeing as how I'm a widow and single mother, but what if I tossed in room and board?"

"Wow, that's quite the incentive," he said.

"I promise to never make you meatloaf again."

"No, promise to always make meatloaf. I love how much I hate it. I'm very complex."

"Deal. But if I'm going to cook for you, you're going to have to sweeten the pot."

"Destination wedding? Say the word and I'll book the flight. I know a guy in Mexico who owes me a favor, and he won't charge much because he's technically legally dead."

"Maybe, but it's bigger than that." She stood on her toes and kissed his jaw.

"Anything. Name your terms," he said, voice more than a little unsteady.

"I need some help weaning a baby. I've tried everything, but recently I heard about a new technique I'm anxious to implement."

He picked her up, bringing her eye level as he pretended to consider. "I find your terms acceptable."

He kissed her.

She kissed him back.

Outside the sun rose on another day, and they lived happily ever after. And sometimes sadly. Occasionally irritably. But always together.

*T*hank you for reading *The Broken and The Brave* in the Spies Like Us series. For more books, please visit my website at www.vanessagraybartal.com

ABOUT THE AUTHOR

Vanessa is a foodie who also loves to write. When she is not trying to find new ways to use sourdough, she likes to troll bakeries and taste test chocolate chip cookies. She lives in rural Ohio with her husband, children, and sheepadoodle. Her life's goal is to fill her books with enough coziness and sunshine to make someone smile. She would love to hear from you, drop her a line on email or facebook.